DREAM DAYS

Essayist and writer for children, Kenneth Grahame was born on 8 March 1859 in Edinburgh, the son of an advocate. The year after his birth Grahame's father was appointed Sherriff-Substitute of Argyllshire and the family moved to Inverary where they remained until 1864 when Grahame's mother died of scarlet fever. He was brought up by his grandmother at Cookham Dene in Berkshire and between 1868 and 1875 he was educated at St Edward's School, Oxford. After a period working for his uncle in London he entered the Bank of England as a gentleman-clerk in 1879.

He became a contributor to W. E. Henley's NATIONAL OBSERVER and to THE YELLOW BOOK and several of his essays were reprinted in Pagan Papers (1893), a collection which owes much to R. L. Stevenson's (q.v.) VIRGINIBUS PUERISQUE. In 1895 he published a second collection THE GOLDEN AGE which was extremely popular and which attracted a favourable critical response from writers like Sir Arthur Quiller-Couch (q.v.) who became a close friend and associate. This was followed by an equally successful sequel, DREAM DAYS in 1898. In both collections the essays and stories are studies of childhood in idyllic rural settings where the adult world of reality is sharply contrasted with the fantasy world of the child. He wrote nothing more until 1908 when he published his best known book THE WIND IN THE WILLOWS, written for his son Alisdair. In this novel for children, which has also given equal pleasure to adults, the arcadian world of the Wild Wood and the River is peopled by an organised society of idealised, peaceful animals: Toad, Rat, Mole, Badger and Otter. Throughout the story runs the timeless symbol of the river, a favourite motif in Grahame's work. It was later made into a popular play, TOAD OF TOAD HALL, by A. A. Milne. In 1916 he edited THE CAMBRIDGE BOOK OF POETRY FOR CHILDREN.

Grahame became Secretary to the Bank of England in 1898 and he married Elspeth Thomson in 1899. He died on 6 July, 1932. His great-grand-uncle was the poet James Grahame (q.v.) and he was the cousin of Anthony Hope (A. H. Hawkins) the author of THE PRISONER OF ZENDA.

Its walls were as of jasper

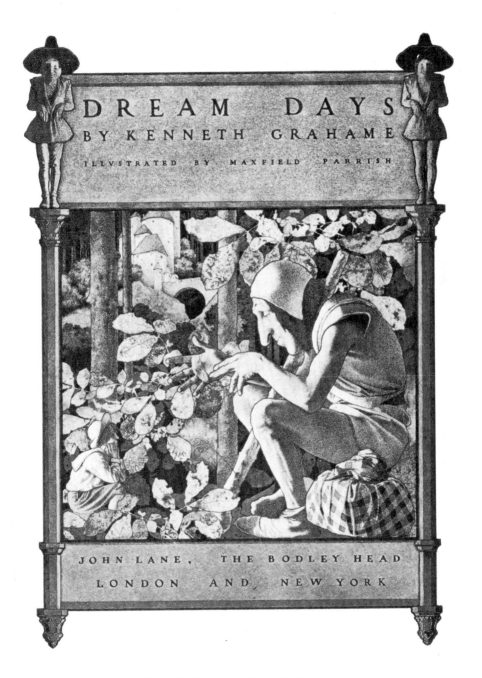

DREAM DAYS

BY KENNETH GRAHAME

ILLUSTRATED BY MAXFIELD PARRISH

JOHN LANE, THE BODLEY HEAD

LONDON AND NEW YORK

Paul Harris Publishing
Edinburgh & New York 1983

First published 1898 by John Lane
This edition first published 1983 by
Paul Harris Publishing
40 York Place, Edinburgh

© Copyright this edition Paul Harris Publishing 1983

ISBN 0 86228 058 3 Cased
ISBN 0 86228 059 1 Limp

The Publishers gratefully acknowledge the financial assistance of
the Scottish Arts Council in the publication of this book.

Printed in Great Britain by A. Wheaton & Company Limited, Exeter

CONTENTS

AND

LIST OF ILLUSTRATIONS

INTRODUCTION

Should a sequel be read by itself, or before one reads it's predecessor? DREAM DAYS follows Kenneth Grahame's THE GOLDEN AGE in direct succession, although there was a three year gap between their dates of publication. THE GOLDEN AGE appeared to bid farewell to the author's evocation of childhood, the adventures and escapades of five young children, but the author rescinded the sentence and took up the tale again.

Both books are catharsis, written not just for delight, but to cleanse the hurt memory of the author. Kenneth Grahame and his sister and brothers had been rejected by their father after their mother's death. They were brought up by a grandmother with other relations in the background who were by no means unkind, but lacking in sympathy, prototypes (though not precise in detail) of the Olympians. Both books are delightful in every part, both are greater as a whole than all the parts put together. Each has its own unity. And so it is possible to begin with DREAM DAYS and ask not 'What happens next?' but 'What happened before?'

The book opens with 'The Twenty First of October', Trafalgar Day and the chosen festival of Selina. The narrator gives a clear and sympathetic account of the particular interests of his older sister, his brother and of himself, an account of which the Olympians remain unaware. A good tutor or governess would have made the discovery and turned it to profit. Lessons are arbitrarily decreed. 'One of us would be singled out, at any moment, freakishly and without regard to his own preferences, to wrestle with the inflections of some idiotic language long rightly dead.'

The unwilling learner would not be aware, the dictators would not think of telling him that one of those languages, far from being idiotic held immortal poetry and the treasures of Greek legend (which they had discovered for themselves in THE GOLDEN AGE). As for the ordinary schoolroom subjects '...common to either sex and held to be necessary ... in geography, for instance, or arithmetic, or the dreary doings of kings and queen — each would have scorned to excel.' Yet left to themselves each of the three older children followed their own way of learning.

Selina's was that of naval history. Edward had a full and accurate knowledge of military uniforms, accoutrements and mottoes and, as for the narrator, his 'own accomplishment took a . . . wider and more untrammelled range . . . did you seek precise information as to the fauna of the American continent, then you had come to the right shop.'

For Selina, the 21st October was a day of celebration. She revives with dramatic force, the glory of Trafalgar, the coming of the news, at once heroic and tragic, of the death of Nelson. She demands: 'Why can't we do something . . . he did everything, why don't we do anything for him?" "Who did everything?" inquired Harold. "Why Nelson of course." "But he's dead isn't he?" "What's that got to do with it?"'

So the children decide to so something. They make a bonfire, a splendid conflagration and the villagers mutter '"Them young devils are at their tricks again."' Brief triumph — but then there are penalties for Selina which she suffers gladly for her hero.

For most of the time Edward is at school but with Harold he meets that noble benefactor The Circus Man. It happens by chance — or by the guidance of some benevolent saint or guardian angel. The chapter begins with a cynical reflection on Olympian lack of honour. They would not forget, those grownups, any of their own engagements, but a promise to children seems to be of little importance. A visit to a circus is proposed and then forgotten as a garden party pushes it out of adult remembrance. Then, unexpectedly, there comes the Circus Man to show them the incredible, forgotten world of 'the magic ring'.

In THE GOLDEN AGE the narrator had set out upon a road that he believes will lead to Rome. An artist tells him of another more wondrous city and they agree to meet there one day in the future. Now it happens that a picture shows him that golden city in the chapter 'Its Walls were of Jasper' and it is seen first by Selina. She claims to be the lady in the blue brocade cloak who sits in the foreground. Edward annexes the man in armour, while Harold selects a man with a wound in his thigh. But the picture cannot give them the reality of the golden city: Edward has to discover it in a book. He has been taken by Aunt Eliza to visit some dull acquaintances, and left to himself, discovers in the library a book which shows him 'my own little city. Its walls are as of jasper with high towers.' In the foreground he sees a river and an island which he might easily reach by rowing boat but the daydream is shattered by the imperious arrival of Aunt Eliza and her fierce denunciation of the book.

There are, though, some grownups who do not grudge books to children. Among them is the Circus Man who makes a beneficial reappearance. It is winter and snow lies on the ground. Snow holds footprints and when Charlotte and the narrator discover dragon's footprints they are compelled to follow their trace. They travel hopefully and lose the prints but their arrival is better than the journey for they have come to the Circus Man's garden. He welcomes them kindly, listens to their story, invites them to tea and shows them his BOOK OF BEASTS. There follows a somewhat different rendering of the legend of St George in 'The Reluctant Dragon', yet when the story-teller has left them, scepticism creeps in. "'Sounded dreadfully like nonsense in parts,'" said Charlotte, only to have the narrator's reply, "'P'raps it's true for all that.'" And the reader is left to decide on the truth or otherwise of a captivating story about a most endearing dragon.

The end of the dream days is near. Sentence is pronounced. Uncle Thomas decrees that the nursery cupboard be cleared of toys and these sent to the Children's Hospital in Putney. The three older children do not mind for they have outgrown toys but Charlotte feels the pain most acutely. They all resent it, though, and they find a way of rescuing the most cherished toys by burying them, secretly, by moonlight, in the corner of the garden. This final episode, this epilogue, is funny, moving and ironic. And it is suffused with an elegaic and poetic quality:

> As we turned to go the man in the moon caught my eye for a moment, and I thought that never had he looked so friendly. He was going to look after them . . . He was always there, more or less, and it was no trouble to him at all, and he would tell them how things were still going up there . . . It made the going away rather easier, to know one had left somebody behind on the spot, a good fellow, too, cheery, comforting . . . a man in whom one had every confidence.

DREAM DAYS ends in tranquility. The catharsis is complete. Together, both books are unique in blending that element with the exuberance of youthful escapades and exploits easily recalled. We may see them not only as masterpieces themselves but as a necessary preparation for Grahame's third and better known classic, THE WIND IN THE WILLOWS. He was to tell it first as a bedtime story for his son Alastair and then to record it for posterity. It is enchanting, happy, the creation of a new, miniature, entrancing world. But could Grahame have created it without having cleansed his hurt soul with the early books?

One of the most alluring games for the booklover is the quest for affinities. There is a kinship between Grahame and Stevenson who did not, alas, live to read any of the books. Stevenson's friend Andrew Lang (1845-1910), who became a friend and admirer of Grahame, has given us glimpses of the golden age and dream days of his own happy boyhood in the Borders. He has told this story indirectly in

INTRODUCTION

some passages of his ADVENTURES AMONG BOOKS. He was one of six children and with the brother next in age to him, he would spend days fishing the Tweed. It was that love that made the long church sermons quite bearable as each boy would make up stories about fishing to while away the long hours of worship. The same Tweedside boyhood is reflected in Lang's best story for children, THE GOLD OF FAIRNIELEE which is set in the years after the Battle of Flodden.

Another affinity is with John Buchan (1875-1940). He too had a Borders boyhood with summers spent with his mother's family in the village of Broughton. His father was a minister of the Free Church of Scotland in Glasgow and a man who was able to balance his strict Calvinism with a love of books, poetry and ballads and the hills and waters surrounding the River Tweed. He too was a fisherman.

One of the essays in Buchan's SCHOLAR GIPSIES (1896) is called 'Nuges Relictae' and it is the sort of farewell to childhood that only a young man could write. Buchan quotes Martial:

Iam tristis nucibus ouer relictis ⸗
Clamoso revocatur a magistro

The Roman boy must put away his playthings at the strident bidding of his tutor. As he moved into that maturity as a writer, Buchan was to find in his own happy childhood, not a refuge or escape, but a source of inspiration for his tales of adventure. Like Grahame he discovered in that childhood the glory of Greek legend and with their heroes made his first journey into 'that realm of gold'.

Grahame has other kindred: a slight one perhaps with Edith Nesbit (1858-1924) who also wrote about a group of high-spirited children; there is Henri Basco (1888-1976) who wrote with a sense of magic and holiness about his childhood in Provence. But, to quote Grahame's own title in THE GOLDEN AGE 'Lusisti Satis', he has gathered for us nuts of gold that will not like the fairy gold of legend turn to withered leaves. DREAM DAYS and THE GOLDEN AGE will continue to hold children from play and their elders from the chimney corner or wherever they happen to be, and to leave them enriched by a diversity of treasures.

Marion Lochhead,
Edinburgh, August 1982

THE TWENTY-FIRST OF OCTOBER

"Harold . . . . with a vision of a frenzied gardener, peastickless, and threatening retribution."

THE TWENTY-FIRST OF OCTOBER

IN the matter of general culture and attainments, we youngsters stood on pretty level ground. True, it was always happening that one of us would be singled out at any moment, freakishly, and without regard to his own preferences, to wrestle with the inflections of some idiotic language long rightly dead; while another, from some fancied artistic tendency which always failed to justify itself, might be told off without warning to hammer out scales and exercises, and to bedew the senseless keys with tears of weariness or of revolt. But in subjects common to either sex, and held to be necessary even for him whose ambition soared no higher than to crack a whip in a circus-ring — in geography, for instance, arithmetic, or the weary doings of kings and queens — each would have scorned to excel. And, indeed, whatever our individual

3

gifts, a general dogged determination to shirk and to evade kept us all at much the same dead level, — a level of ignorance tempered by insubordination.

Fortunately there existed a wide range of subjects, of healthier tone than those already enumerated, in which we were free to choose for ourselves, and which we would have scorned to consider education; and in these we freely followed each his own particular line, often attaining an amount of special knowledge which struck our ignorant elders as simply uncanny. For Edward, the uniforms, accoutrements, colours, and mottoes of the regiments composing the British Army had a special glamour. In the matter of facings he was simply faultless; among chevrons, badges, medals, and stars, he moved familiarly; he even knew the names of most of the colonels in command; and he would squander sunny hours prone on the lawn, heedless of challenge from bird or beast, poring over a tattered Army List. My own accomplishment was of another character — took, as it seemed to me, a wider and a more

untrammelled range. Dragoons might have
swaggered in Lincoln green, riflemen might
have donned sporrans over tartan trews, without exciting notice or comment from me. But
did you seek precise information as to the fauna
of the American continent, then you had come
to the right shop. Where and why the bison
" wallowed " ; how beaver were to be trapped
and wild turkeys stalked ; the grizzly and how
to handle him, and the pretty pressing ways of
the constrictor, — in fine, the haunts and the
habits of all that burrowed, strutted, roared, or
wriggled between the Atlantic and the Pacific,
— all this knowledge I took for my province.
By the others my equipment was fully recognised. Supposing a book with a bear-hunt in
it made its way into the house, and the atmosphere was electric with excitement ; still, it was
necessary that I should first decide whether the
slot had been properly described and properly
followed up, ere the work could be stamped
with full approval. A writer might have won
fame throughout the civilised globe for his
trappers and his realistic backwoods, and all

went for nothing. If his pemmican were not properly compounded I damned his achievement, and it was heard no more of.

Harold was hardly old enough to possess a special subject of his own. He had his instincts, indeed, and at bird's-nesting they almost amounted to prophecy. Where we others only suspected eggs, surmised possible eggs, hinted doubtfully at eggs in the neighbourhood, Harold went straight for the right bush, bough, or hole as if he carried a divining-rod. But this faculty belonged to the class of mere gifts, and was not to be ranked with Edward's lore regarding facings, and mine as to the habits of prairie-dogs, both gained by painful study and extensive travel in those "realms of gold," the Army List and Ballantyne.

Selina's subject, quite unaccountably, happened to be naval history. There is no laying down rules as to subjects; you just possess them — or rather, they possess you — and their genesis or protoplasm is rarely to be tracked down. Selina had never so much as seen the sea; but for that matter neither had I ever set foot on the American continent, the by-ways of which I knew so intimately. And just as I, if set down without warning in the middle of the Rocky Mountains, would have been perfectly at home, so Selina, if a genie had dropped her suddenly on Portsmouth Hard, could have given points to most of its frequenters. From the days of Blake down to the death of Nelson (she never condescended further) Selina had taken spiritual part in every notable engagement of the British Navy; and even in the dark days when she had to pick up skirts and flee, chased by an ungallant De Ruyter or Van Tromp, she was yet cheerful in the consciousness that ere long she would be gleefully hammering the fleets of the world, in the glorious times to follow. When that golden period arrived, Selina was busy indeed; and, while loving best to stand where the splinters were flying the thickest, she was also a careful and critical student of seamanship and of manœuvre. She knew the order in which the great line-of-battle ships moved into action, the vessels they respectively engaged, the moment when each

7

let go its anchor, and which of them had a spring on its cable (while not understanding the phrase, she carefully noted the fact); and she habitually went into an engagement on the quarter-deck of the gallant ship that reserved its fire the longest.

At the time of Selina's weird seizure I was unfortunately away from home, on a loathsome visit to an aunt; and my account is therefore feebly compounded from hearsay. It was an absence I never ceased to regret — scoring it up, with a sense of injury, against the aunt. There was a splendid uselessness about the whole performance that specially appealed to my artistic sense. That it should have been Selina, too, who should break out this way — Selina, who had just become a regular sub-scriber to the " Young Ladies' Journal," and who allowed herself to be taken out to strange teas with an air of resignation palpably assumed — this was a special joy, and served to remind me that much of this dreaded convention that was creeping over us might be, after all, only veneer. Edward also was absent, getting licked

into shape at school; but to him the loss was
nothing. With his stern practical bent he
would n't have seen any sense in it — to recall
one of his favourite expressions. To Harold,
however, for whom the gods had always cherished a special tenderness, it was granted, not
only to witness, but also, priestlike, to feed the
sacred fire itself. And if at the time he paid
the penalty exacted by the sordid unimaginative
ones who temporarily rule the roast, he must
ever after, one feels sure, have carried inside
him some of the white gladness of the acolyte
who, greatly privileged, has been permitted
to swing a censer at the sacring of the very
Mass.

October was mellowing fast, and with it the
year itself; full of tender hints, in woodland
and hedgerow, of a course well-nigh completed.
From all sides that still afternoon you caught
the quick breathing and sob of the runner
nearing the goal. Preoccupied and possessed,
Selina had strayed down the garden and out
into the pasture beyond, where, on a bit of
rising ground that dominated the garden on

one side and the downs with the old coach-road on the other, she had cast herself down to chew the cud of fancy. There she was presently joined by Harold, breathless and very full of his latest grievance.

"I asked him not to," he burst out. "I said if he'd only please wait a bit and Edward would be back soon, and it couldn't matter to *him*, and the pig wouldn't mind, and Edward'd be pleased and everybody'd be happy. But he just said he was very sorry, but bacon didn't wait for nobody. So I told him he was a regular beast, and then I came away. And — and I b'lieve they're doing it now!"

"Yes, he's a beast," agreed Selina, absently. She had forgotten all about the pig-killing. Harold kicked away a freshly thrown-up mole-hill, and prodded down the hole with a stick. From the direction of Farmer Larkin's demesne came a long-drawn note of sorrow, a thin cry and appeal, telling that the stout soul of a black Berkshire pig was already faring down the stony track to Hades.

"D'you know what day it is?" said Selina

presently, in a low voice, looking far away before her.

Harold did not appear to know, nor yet to care. He had laid open his mole-run for a yard or so, and was still grubbing at it absorbedly.

"It's Trafalgar Day," went on Selina, trancedly; "Trafalgar Day — and nobody cares!"

Something in her tone told Harold that he was not behaving quite becomingly. He didn't exactly know in what manner; still, he abandoned his mole-hunt for a more courteous attitude of attention.

"Over there," resumed Selina — she was gazing out in the direction of the old highroad — "over there the coaches used to go by. Uncle Thomas was telling me about it the other day. And the people used to watch for 'em coming, to tell the time by, and p'r'aps to get their parcels. And one morning — they wouldn't be expecting anything different — one morning, first there would be a cloud of dust, as usual, and then the coach would come racing by, and *then* they would know! For the coach would be dressed in laurel, all laurel from stem to stern! And the coachman would be wearing laurel, and the guard would be wearing laurel, and then they would know, then they would know!"

Harold listened in respectful silence. He would much rather have been hunting the mole, who must have been a mile away by this time if he had his wits about him. But he had all the natural instincts of a gentleman; of whom it is one of the principal marks, if not the complete definition, never to show signs of being bored.

Selina rose to her feet, and paced the turf restlessly with a short quarter-deck walk.

"Why can't we *do* something?" she burst out presently. "*He* — he did everything — why can't we do anything for him?"

"*Who* did everything?" inquired Harold, meekly. It was useless wasting further longings on that mole. Like the dead, he travelled fast.

"Why, Nelson, of course," said Selina, shortly, still looking restlessly around for help or suggestion.

"But he's — he's *dead*, is n't he?" asked Harold, slightly puzzled.

"What's that got to do with it?" retorted his sister, resuming her caged-lion promenade.

Harold was somewhat taken aback. In the case of the pig, for instance, whose last outcry had now passed into stillness, he had considered the chapter as finally closed. Whatever innocent mirth the holidays might hold in store for Edward, that particular pig, at least, would not be a contributor. And now he was given to understand that the situation had not materially changed! He would have to revise his ideas, it seemed. Sitting up on end, he looked towards the garden for assistance in the task. Thence, even as he gazed, a tiny column of smoke rose straight up into the still air. The gardener had been sweeping that afternoon, and now, an unconscious priest, was offering his sacrifice of autumn leaves to the calm-eyed goddess of changing hues and chill forebodings who was moving slowly about the land that golden afternoon. Harold was up and off in a moment, forgetting Nelson, forgetting the pig, the mole, the Larkin betrayal, and Selina's strange fever of conscience. Here was fire, real fire, to play with, and that was even better than messing with water, or remodelling the plastic surface of the earth. Of all the toys the world provides for right-minded persons, the original elements rank easily the first.

But Selina sat on where she was, her chin on her fists; and her fancies whirled and drifted, here and there, in curls and eddies, along with the smoke she was watching. As the quick-footed dusk of the short October day stepped lightly over the garden, little red tongues of fire might be seen to leap and vanish in the smoke. Harold, anon staggering under armfuls of leaves, anon stoking vigorously, was discernible only at fitful intervals. It was another sort of smoke that the inner eye of Selina was looking upon, — a smoke that hung in sullen banks round the masts and the hulls of the fighting ships; a smoke from beneath which came thunder and the crash and the splinter-rip, the shout of the boarding-party, the choking sob of the gunner stretched by his gun; a smoke from out of which at last she saw, as through a riven pall, the radiant spirit of the Victor, crowned with the coronal of a perfect death, leap in full assurance up into the ether that Immortals breathe. The dusk was glooming towards darkness when she rose and moved slowly down towards the beckoning fire; something of the priestess in her stride, something of the devotee in the set purpose of her eye.

The leaves were well alight by this time, and Harold had just added an old furze bush, which flamed and crackled stirringly.

" Go 'n' get some more sticks," ordered Selina, " and shavings, 'n' chunks of wood, 'n' anything you can find. Look here — in the kitchen-garden there's a pile of old pea-sticks. Fetch as many as you can carry, and then go back and bring some more! "

" But I say, — " began Harold, amazedly, scarce knowing his sister, and with a vision of a frenzied gardener, pea-stickless and threatening retribution.

" Go and fetch 'em quick! " shouted Selina, stamping with impatience.

Harold ran off at once, true to the stern system of discipline in which he had been nurtured. But his eyes were like round O's, and as he ran he talked fast to himself, in evident disorder of mind.

The pea-sticks made a rare blaze, and the fire, no longer smouldering sullenly, leapt up and began to assume the appearance of a genuine bonfire. Harold, awed into silence at first, began to jump round it with shouts of triumph. Selina looked on grimly, with knitted brow; she was not yet fully satisfied. " Can't you get any more sticks?" she said presently. " Go and hunt about. Get some old hampers and matting and things out of the tool-house. Smash up that old cucumber frame Edward shoved you into, the day we were playing scouts and Mohicans. Stop a bit! Hooray! I know. You come along with me."

Hard by there was a hot-house, Aunt Eliza's special pride and joy, and even grimly approved of by the gardener. At one end, in an outhouse adjoining, the necessary firing was stored ; and to this sacred fuel, of which we were strictly forbidden to touch a stick, Selina went straight. Harold followed obediently, prepared for any crime after that of the pea-sticks, but pinching himself to see if he were really awake.

"You bring some coals," said Selina briefly, without any palaver or pro-and-con discussion. "Here's a basket. *I'll* manage the faggots!"

In a very few minutes there was little doubt about its being a genuine bonfire and no paltry makeshift. Selina, a Mænad now, hatless and tossing disordered locks, all the dross of the young lady purged out of her, stalked around the pyre of her own purloining, or prodded it with a pea-stick. And as she prodded she murmured at intervals, "I *knew* there was something we could do! It isn't much — but still it's *something!*"

The gardener had gone home to his tea. Aunt Eliza had driven out for hers a long way off, and was not expected back till quite late; and this far end of the garden was not overlooked by any windows. So the Tribute blazed on merrily unchecked. Villagers far away, catching sight of the flare, muttered something about "them young devils at their tricks again," and trudged on beer-wards. Never a thought of what day it was, never a thought for Nelson, who preserved their honest pint-pots, to be paid for in honest pence, and saved them from *litres* and decimal coinage. Nearer at hand, frightened rabbits popped up and vanished with a flick of white tails ; scared birds fluttered among the branches, or sped across the glade to quieter sleeping-quarters ; but never a bird nor a beast gave a thought to the hero to whom they owed it that each year their little homes of horsehair, wool, or moss, were safe stablished 'neath the flap of the British flag ; and that Game Laws, quietly permanent, made *la chasse* a terror only to their betters. No one seemed to know, nor to care, nor to sympathise. In all the ecstasy of her burnt-offering and sacrifice, Selina stood alone.

And yet — not quite alone ! For, as the fire was roaring at its best, certain stars stepped delicately forth on the surface of the immensity above, and peered down doubtfully — with wonder at first, then with interest, then with recog-

nition, with a start of glad surprise. *They* at
least knew all about it, *they* understood. Among
them the Name was a daily familiar word; his
story was a part of the music to which they
swung, himself was their fellow and their mate
and comrade. So they peeped, and winked,
and peeped again, and called to their laggard
brothers to come quick and see.

.   .   .   .

"The best of life is but intoxication;" and
Selina, who during her brief inebriation had
lived in an ecstasy as golden as our drab existence affords, had to experience the inevitable
bitterness of awakening sobriety, when the dy-
ing down of the flames into sullen embers coin-
cided with the frenzied entrance of Aunt Eliza
on the scene. It was not so much that she was
at once and forever disrated, broke, sent before
the mast, and branded as one on whom no reli-
ance could be placed, even with Edward safe
at school, and myself under the distant vigilance
of an aunt; that her pocket money was stopped
indefinitely, and her new Church Service, the
pride of her last birthday, removed from her

own custody and placed under the control of a Trust. She sorrowed rather because she had dragged poor Harold, against his better judgment, into a most horrible scrape, and moreover because, when the reaction had fairly set in, when the exaltation had fizzled away and the young-lady portion of her had crept timorously back to its wonted lodging, she could only see herself as a plain fool, unjustified, undeniable, without a shadow of an excuse or explanation.

As for Harold, youth and a short memory made his case less pitiful than it seemed to his more sensitive sister. True, he started upstairs to his lonely cot bellowing dismally, before him a dreary future of pains and penalties, sufficient to last to the crack of doom. Outside his door, however, he tumbled over Augustus the cat, and made capture of him; and at once his mourning was changed into a song of triumph, as he conveyed his prize into port. For Augustus, who detested above all things going to bed with little boys, was ever more knave than fool, and the trapper who was wily enough to ensnare him had achieved something notable.

Augustus, when he realised that his fate was sealed, and his night's lodging settled, wisely made the best of things, and listened, with a languorous air of complete comprehension, to the incoherent babble concerning pigs and heroes, moles and bonfires, which served Harold for a self-sung lullaby. Yet it may be doubted whether Augustus was one of those rare fellows who thoroughly understood.

But Selina knew no more of this source of consolation than of the sympathy with which the stars were winking above her; and it was only after some sad interval of time, and on a very moist pillow, that she drifted into that quaint inconsequent country where you may meet your own pet hero strolling down the road, and commit what hair-brained oddities you like, and everybody understands and appreciates.

DIES IRÆ

"And, last of all, you - you, the General, the fabled hero - you would enter, on your coal-black charge, your pale set face seamed by an interesting sabre-cut."

DIES IRÆ

THOSE memorable days that move in procession, their heads just out of the mist
of years long dead — the most of them are full-
eyed as the dandelion that from dawn to shade
has steeped itself in sunlight. Here and there
in their ranks, however, moves a forlorn one
who is blind — blind in the sense of the dulled
window-pane on which the pelting raindrops
have mingled and run down, obscuring sunshine
and the circling birds, happy fields, and storied
garden; blind with the spatter of a misery un-
comprehended, unanalysed, only felt as something corporeal in its buffeting effects.

Martha began it; and yet Martha was not
really to blame. Indeed, that was half the
trouble of it — no solid person stood full in
view, to be blamed and to make atonement.
There was only a wretched, impalpable condi-

tion to deal with. Breakfast was just over;
the sun was summoning us, imperious as a
herald with clamour of trumpet; I ran upstairs
to her with a broken bootlace in my hand, and
there she was, crying in a corner, her head in
her apron. Nothing could be got from her but
the same dismal succession of sobs that would
not have done, that struck and hurt like a
physical beating; and meanwhile the sun was
getting impatient, and I wanted my bootlace.

Inquiry below stairs revealed the cause.
Martha's brother was dead, it seemed — her
sailor brother Billy; drowned in one of those
strange far-off seas it was our dream to navigate
one day. We had known Billy well, and appreciated him. When an approaching visit of Billy
to his sister had been announced, we had counted
the days to it. When his cheery voice was at
last heard in the kitchen and we had descended
with shouts, first of all he had to exhibit his
tattooed arms, always a subject for fresh delight
and envy and awe; then he was called upon for
tricks, jugglings, and strange, fearful gymnas-
tics; and lastly came yarns, and more yarns,

and yarns till bedtime. There had never been any one like Billy in his own particular sphere; and now he was drowned, they said, and Martha was miserable, and — and I couldn't get a new bootlace. They told me that Billy would never come back any more, and I stared out of the window at the sun which came back, right enough, every day, and their news conveyed nothing whatever to me. Martha's sorrow hit home a little, but only because the actual sight and sound of it gave me a dull, bad sort of pain low down inside — a pain not to be actually located. Moreover, I was still wanting my bootlace.

This was a poor sort of a beginning to a day that, so far as outside conditions went, had promised so well. I rigged up a sort of jury-mast of a bootlace with a bit of old string, and wandered off to look up the girls, conscious of a jar and a discordance in the scheme of things. The moment I entered the schoolroom something in the air seemed to tell me that here, too, matters were strained and awry. Selina was staring listlessly out of the window, one foot curled round her leg. When I spoke to her she jerked a shoulder testily, but did not condescend to the civility of a reply. Charlotte, absolutely unoccupied, sprawled in a chair, and there were signs of sniffles about her, even at that early hour. It was but a trifling matter that had caused all this electricity in the atmosphere, and the girls' manner of taking it seemed to me most unreasonable. Within the last few days the time had come round for the despatch of a hamper to Edward at school. Only one hamper a term was permitted him, so its preparation was a sort of blend of revelry and religious ceremony. After the main corpus of the thing had been carefully selected and safely bestowed — the pots of jam, the cake, the sausages, and the apples that filled up corners so nicely — after the last package had been wedged in, the girls had deposited their own private and personal offerings on the top. I forget their precise nature; anyhow, they were nothing of any particular practical use to a boy. But they had involved some contrivance and labour, some skimping of pocket money, and much delightful

cloud-building as to the effect on their enraptured
recipient. Well, yesterday there had come a
terse acknowledgment from Edward, heartily
commending the cakes and the jam, stamping
the sausages with the seal of Smith major's
approval, and finally hinting that, fortified as
he now was, nothing more was necessary but
a remittance of five shillings in postage stamps
to enable him to face the world armed against
every buffet of fate. That was all. Never a
word or a hint of the personal tributes or of his
appreciation of them. To us — to Harold and
me, that is — the letter seemed natural and sensible enough. After all, provender was the
main thing, and five shillings stood for a complete equipment against the most unexpected
turns of luck. The presents were very well in
their way — very nice, and so on — but life was
a serious matter, and the contest called for cakes
and half-crowns to carry it on, not gew-gaws
and knitted mittens and the like. The girls, however, in their obstinate way, persisted in taking
their own view of the slight. Hence it was that
I received my second rebuff of the morning.

Somewhat disheartened, I made my way downstairs and out into the sunlight, where I found Harold playing conspirators by himself on the gravel. He had dug a small hole in the walk and had laid an imaginary train of powder thereto ; and, as he sought refuge in the laurels from the inevitable explosion, I heard him murmur: " ' My God!' said the Czar, 'my plans are frustrated!' " It seemed an excellent occasion for being a black puma. Harold liked black pumas, on the whole, as well as any animal we were familiar with. So I launched myself on him, with the appropriate howl, rolling him over on the gravel.

Life may be said to be composed of things that come off and things that don't come off. This thing, unfortunately, was one of the things that did n't come off. From beneath me I heard a shrill cry of, " Oh, it 's my sore knee! " And Harold wriggled himself free from the puma's clutches, bellowing dismally. Now, I honestly did n't know he had a sore knee, and, what 's more, he knew I did n't know he had a sore knee. According to boy-ethics, therefore, his attitude was wrong, sore knee or not, and no apology was due from me. I made half-way advances, however, suggesting we should lie in ambush by the edge of the pond and cut off the ducks as they waddled down in simple, unsuspecting single file ; then hunt them as bisons flying scattered over the vast prairie. A fascinating pursuit this, and strictly illicit. But Harold would none of my overtures, and retreated to the house wailing with full lungs.

Things were getting simply infernal. I struck out blindly for the open country ; and even as I made for the gate a shrill voice from a window bade me keep off the flower-beds. When the gate had swung to behind me with a vicious click I felt better, and after ten minutes along the road it began to grow on me that some radical change was needed, that I was in a blind alley, and that this intolerable state of things must somehow cease. All that I could do I had already done. As well-meaning a fellow as ever stepped was pounding along the road that day, with an exceeding sore heart ; one who only wished to live and let live, in touch with his fellows, and appreciating what joys life had to offer. What was wanted now was a complete change of environment. Somewhere in the world, I felt sure, justice and sympathy still resided. There were places called pampas, for instance, that sounded well. League upon league of grass, with just an occasional wild horse, and not a relation within the horizon! To a bruised spirit this seemed a sane and a healing sort of existence. There were other pleasant corners, again, where you dived for pearls and stabbed sharks in the stomach with your big knife. No relations would be likely to come interfering with you when thus blissfully occupied. And yet I did not wish — just yet — to have done with relations entirely. They should be made to feel their position first, to see themselves as they really were, and to wish — when it was too late — that they had behaved more properly.

Of all professions, the army seemed to lend itself the most thoroughly to the scheme. You enlisted, you followed the drum, you marched, fought, and ported arms, under strange skies,

through unrecorded years. At last, at long
last, your opportunity would come, when the
horrors of war were flickering through the quiet
country-side where you were cradled and bred,
but where the memory of you had long been dim.
Folk would run together, clamorous, palsied
with fear ; and among the terror-stricken groups
would figure certain aunts. "What hope is
left us?" they would ask themselves, "save in
the clemency of the General, the mysterious,
invincible General, of whom men tell such
romantic tales?" And the army would march
in, and the guns would rattle and leap along the
village street, and, last of all, you — you, the
General, the fabled hero — you would enter, on
your coal-black charger, your pale set face
seamed by an interesting sabre-cut. And then
— but every boy has rehearsed this familiar
piece a score of times. You are magnanimous,
in fine — that goes without saying , you have
a coal-black horse, and a sabre-cut, and you
can afford to be very magnanimous. But all
the same you give them a good talking-to.

This pleasant conceit simply ravished my

soul for some twenty minutes, and then the old
sense of injury began to well up afresh, and to
call for new plasters and soothing syrups. This
time I took refuge in happy thoughts of the sea.
The sea was my real sphere, after all. On the
sea, in especial, you could combine distinction
with lawlessness, whereas the army seemed to
be always weighted by a certain plodding sub-
mission to discipline. To be sure, by all
accounts, the life was at first a rough one. But
just then I wanted to suffer keenly ; I wanted
to be a poor devil of a cabin boy, kicked, beaten,
and sworn at — for a time. Perhaps some hint,
some inkling of my sufferings might reach their
ears. In due course the sloop or felucca would
turn up — it always did — the rakish-looking
craft, black of hull, low in the water, and brist-
ling with guns ; the jolly Roger flapping overhead, and myself for sole commander. By and
by, as usually happened, an East Indiaman
would come sailing along full of relations — not
a necessary relation would be missing. And
the crew should walk the plank, and the captain
should dance from his own yard-arm, and then

DIES IRÆ

I would take the passengers in hand — that miserable group of well-known figures cowering on the quarter-deck ! — and then — and then the same old performance : the air thick with magnanimity. In all the repertory of heroes, none is more truly magnanimous than your pirate chief.

When at last I brought myself back from the future to the actual present, I found that these delectable visions had helped me over a longer stretch of road than I had imagined ; and I looked around and took my bearings. To the right of me was a long low building of grey stone, new, and yet not smugly so ; new, and yet possessing distinction, marked with a character that did not depend on lichen or on crumbling semi-effacement of moulding and mullion. Strangers might have been puzzled to classify it ; to me, an explorer from earliest years, the place was familiar enough. Most folk called it "The Settlement" ; others, with quite sufficient conciseness for our neighbourhood, spoke of "them there fellows up by Halliday's" ; others again, with a hint of derision, named

them the "monks." This last title I supposed
to be intended for satire, and knew to be fatu-
ously wrong. I was thoroughly acquainted with
monks — in books — and well knew the cut of
their long frocks, their shaven polls, and their
fascinating big dogs, with brandy-bottles round
their necks, incessantly hauling happy travellers
out of the snow. The only dog at the settlement was an Irish terrier, and the good fellows
who owned him, and were owned by him, in
common, wore clothes of the most nondescript
order, and mostly cultivated side-whiskers. I
had wandered up there one day, searching (as
usual) for something I never found, and had
been taken in by them and treated as friend and
comrade. They had made me free of their ideal
little rooms, full of books and pictures, and clean
of the antimacassar taint ; they had shown me
their chapel, high, hushed, and faintly scented,
beautiful with a strange new beauty born both
of what it had and what it had not — that too
familiar dowdiness of common places of worship. They had also fed me in their dining-hall,
where a long table stood on trestles plain to

view, and all the woodwork was natural, un-
painted, healthily scrubbed, and redolent of the
forest it came from. I brought away from that
visit, and kept by me for many days, a sense of
cleanness, of the freshness that pricks the senses
— the freshness of cool spring water ; and the
large swept spaces of the rooms, the red tiles,
and the oaken settles, suggested a comfort that
had no connexion with padded upholstery.

On this particular morning I was in much
too unsociable a mind for paying friendly calls.
Still, something in the aspect of the place har-
monised with my humour, and I worked my
way round to the back, where the ground, after
affording level enough for a kitchen-garden,
broke steeply away. Both the word Gothic
and the thing itself were still unknown to me ;
yet doubtless the architecture of the place, con-
sistent throughout, accounted for its sense of
comradeship in my hour of disheartenment. As
I mused there, with the low, grey, purposeful-
looking building before me, and thought of my
pleasant friends within, and what good times
they always seemed to be having, and how they

37

larked with the Irish terrier, whose footing was one of a perfect equality, I thought of a certain look in their faces, as if they had a common purpose and a business, and were acting under orders thoroughly recognised and understood. I remembered, too, something that Martha had told me, about these same fellows doing "a power o' good," and other hints I had collected vaguely, of renouncements, rules, self-denials, and the like. Thereupon, out of the depths of my morbid soul swam up a new and fascinating idea; and at once the career of arms seemed over-acted and stale, and piracy, as a profession, flat and unprofitable. This, then, or something like it, should be my vocation and my revenge. A severer line of business, perhaps, such as I had read of; something that included black bread and a hair-shirt. There should be vows, too — irrevocable, blood-curdling vows; and an iron grating. This iron grating was the most necessary feature of all, for I intended that on the other side of it my relations should range themselves — I mentally ran over the catalogue, and saw that the whole gang was present, all in their proper places — a sad-eyed row, combined in tristful appeal. "We see our error now," they would say; "we were always dull dogs, slow to catch — especially in those akin to us — the finer qualities of soul! We misunderstood you, misappreciated you, and we own up to it. And now — " "Alas, my dear friends," I would strike in here, waving towards them an ascetic hand — one of the emaciated sort, that lets the light shine through at the finger-tips — "Alas, you come too late! This conduct is fitting and meritorious on your part, and indeed I always expected it of you, sooner or later; but the die is cast, and you may go home again and bewail at your leisure this too tardy repentance of yours. For me, I am vowed and dedicated, and my relations henceforth are austerity and holy works. Once a month, should you wish it, it shall be your privilege to come and gaze at me through this very solid grating; but — " *Whack!*

A well-aimed clod of garden soil, whizzing just past my ear, starred on a tree-trunk behind, spattering me with dirt. The present came

back to me in a flash, and I nimbly took cover
behind the trees, realising that the enemy was
up and abroad, with ambuscades, alarms, and
thrilling sallies. It was the gardener's boy, I
knew well enough ; a red proletariat, who hated
me just because I was a gentleman. Hastily
picking up a nice sticky clod in one hand, with
the other I delicately projected my hat beyond
the shelter of the tree-trunk. I had not fought
with Red-skins all these years for nothing.

As I had expected, another clod, of the first
class for size and stickiness, took my poor hat
full in the centre. Then, Ajax-like, shouting
terribly, I issued from shelter and discharged
my ammunition. Woe then for the gardener's
boy, who, unprepared, skipping in premature
triumph, took the clod full in his stomach ! He,
the foolish one, witless on whose side the gods
were fighting that day, discharged yet other
missiles, wavering and wide of the mark ; for
his wind had been taken with the first clod, and
he shot wildly, as one already desperate and in
flight. I got another clod in at short range ;
we clinched on the brow of the hill, and rolled

down to the bottom together. When he had shaken himself free and regained his legs, he trotted smartly off in the direction of his mother's cottage ; but over his shoulder he discharged at me both imprecation and deprecation, menace mixed up with an under-current of tears.

But as for me, I made off smartly for the road, my frame tingling, my head high, with never a backward look at the Settlement of suggestive aspect, or at my well-planned future which lay in fragments around it. Life had its jollities, then ; life was action, contest, victory ! The present was rosy once more, surprises lurked on every side, and I was beginning to feel villainously hungry.

Just as I gained the road a cart came rattling by, and I rushed for it, caught the chain that hung below, and swung thrillingly between the dizzy wheels, choked and blinded with delicious-smelling dust, the world slipping by me like a streaky ribbon below, till the driver licked at me with his whip, and I had to descend to earth again. Abandoning the beaten track, I then struck homewards through the fields ; not that

the way was very much shorter, but rather because on that route one avoided the bridge, and
had to splash through the stream and get refresh-
ingly wet. Bridges were made for narrow folk,
for people with aims and vocations which compelled abandonment of many of life's highest
pleasures. Truly wise men called on each element alike to minister to their joy, and while the
touch of sun-bathed air, the fragrance of garden
soil, the ductible qualities of mud, and the
spark-whirling rapture of playing with fire, had
each their special charm, they did not overlook
the bliss of getting their feet wet. As I came
forth on the common Harold broke out of an
adjoining copse and ran to meet me, the morning rain-clouds all blown away from his face.
He had made a new squirrel-stick, it seemed.
Made it all himself; melted the lead and everything! I examined the instrument critically,
and pronounced it absolutely magnificent. As
we passed in at our gate the girls were distantly
visible, gardening with a zeal in cheerful con-
trast to their heartsick lassitude of the morning.
"There's bin another letter come to-day,"

Harold explained, " and the hamper got joggled about on the journey, and the presents worked down into the straw and all over the place. One of 'em turned up inside the cold duck. And that's why they weren't found at first. And Edward said, Thanks *awfully!* "

I did not see Martha again until we were all re-assembled at tea-time, when she seemed red-eyed and strangely silent, neither scolding nor finding fault with anything. Instead, she was very kind and thoughtful with jams and things, feverishly pressing unwonted delicacies on us, who wanted little pressing enough. Then suddenly, when I was busiest, she disappeared; and Charlotte whispered me presently that she had heard her go to her room and lock herself in. This struck me as a funny sort of proceeding.

MUTABILE SEMPER

"You go up the steps, and in at the door, and the very first place you come to is the Chocolate Room!"

MUTABILE SEMPER

SHE stood on the other side of the garden fence, and regarded me gravely as I came down the road. Then she said, "Hi-o!" and I responded, "Hullo!" and pulled up somewhat nervously.

To tell the truth, the encounter was not entirely unexpected on my part. The previous Sunday I had seen her in church, and after service it had transpired who she was, this newcomer, and what aunt she was staying with. That morning a volunteer had been called for, to take a note to the Parsonage, and rather to my own surprise I had found myself stepping forward with alacrity, while the others had become suddenly absorbed in various pursuits, or had sneaked unobtrusively out of view. Certainly I had not yet formed any deliberate plan of action; yet I suppose I recollected that the road to the Parsonage led past her aunt's garden.

She began the conversation, while I hopped backwards and forwards over the ditch, feigning a careless ease.

" Saw you in church on Sunday," she said ; " only you looked different then. All dressed up, and your hair quite smooth, and brushed up at the sides, and oh, so shiny ! What do they put on it to make it shine like that ? Don't you hate having your hair brushed?" she ran on, without waiting for an answer. " How your boots squeaked when you came down the aisle ! When mine squeak, I walk in all the puddles till they stop. Think I 'll get over the fence."

This she proceeded to do in a business-like way, while, with my hands deep in my pockets, I regarded her movements with silent interest, as those of some strange new animal.

" I 've been gardening," she explained, when she had joined me, " but I didn't like it. There's so many worms about to-day. I hate worms. Wish they'd keep out of the way when I 'm digging."

"Oh, I like worms when I'm digging," I replied heartily, "seem to make things more lively, don't they?"

She reflected. "Should n't mind 'em so much if they were warm and *dry*," she said, "but—" here she shivered, and somehow I liked her for it, though if it had been my own flesh and blood hoots of derision would have instantly assailed her.

From worms we passed, naturally enough, to frogs, and thence to pigs, aunts, gardeners, rocking-horses, and other fellow-citizens of our common kingdom. In five minutes we had each other's confidences, and I seemed to have known her for a lifetime. Somehow, on the subject of one's self it was easier to be frank and communicative with her than with one's female kin. It must be, I supposed, because she was less familiar with one's faulty, tattered past.

"I was watching you as you came along the road," she said presently, "and you had your head down and your hands in your pockets, and you were n't throwing stones at anything, or whistling, or jumping over things; and I thought perhaps you'd bin scolded, or got a stomach-ache."

"No," I answered shyly, "it wasn't that. Fact is, I was — I often — but it's a secret."

There I made an error in tactics. That enkindling word set her dancing round me, half beseeching, half imperious. "Oh, do tell it me!" she cried. "You must! I'll never tell anyone else at all, I vow and declare I won't!"

Her small frame wriggled with emotion, and with imploring eyes she jigged impatiently just in front of me. Her hair was tumbled bewitchingly on her shoulders, and even the loss of a front tooth — a loss incidental to her age — seemed but to add a piquancy to her face.

"You won't care to hear about it," I said, wavering. "Besides, I can't explain exactly. I think I won't tell you." But all the time I knew I should have to.

"But I *do* care," she wailed plaintively. "I didn't think you'd be so unkind!"

This would never do. That little downward tug at either corner of the mouth — I knew the symptom only too well!

"It's like this," I began stammeringly. "This bit of road here — up as far as that corner — you know it's a horrid dull bit of road. I'm always having to go up and down it, and I know it so well, and I'm so sick of it. So whenever I get to that corner, I just — well, I go right off to another place!"

"What sort of a place?" she asked, looking round her gravely.

"Of course it's just a place I imagine," I went on hurriedly and rather shamefacedly: "but it's an awfully nice place — the nicest place you ever saw. And I always go off there in church, or during joggraphy lessons."

"I'm sure it's not nicer than my home," she cried patriotically. "Oh, you ought to see my home — it's lovely! We've got — "

"Yes it is, ever so much nicer," I interrupted. "I mean" — I went on apologetically — "of course I know your home's beautiful and all that. But this *must* be nicer, 'cos if you want anything at all, you've only *got* to want it, and you can have it!"

"That sounds jolly," she murmured. "Tell

me more about it, please. Tell me how you get there, first."

" I — don't — quite — know — exactly," I replied. " I just go. But generally it begins by — well, you 're going up a broad, clear river in a sort of a boat. You 're not rowing or anything — you 're just moving along. And there 's beautiful grass meadows on both sides, and the river 's very full, quite up to the level of the grass. And you glide along by the edge. And the people are haymaking there, and playing games, and walking about ; and they shout to you, and you shout back to them, and they bring you things to eat out of their baskets, and let you drink out of their bottles ; and some of 'em are the nice people you read about in books. And so at last you come to the Palace steps — great broad marble steps, reaching right down to the water. And there at the steps you find every sort of boat you can imagine — schooners, and punts, and row-boats, and little men-of-war. And you have any sort of boating you want to — rowing, or sailing, or shoving about in a punt ! "

MUTABILE SEMPER

"I'd go sailing," she said decidedly: "and I'd steer. No, *you'd* have to steer, and I'd sit about on the deck. No, I wouldn't though; I'd row — at least I'd make you row, and I'd steer. And then we'd — Oh, no! I'll tell you what we'd do! We'd just sit in a punt and dabble!"

"Of course we'll do just what you like," I said hospitably; but already I was beginning to feel my liberty of action somewhat curtailed by this exigent visitor I had so rashly admitted into my sanctum.

"I don't think we'd boat at all," she finally decided. "It's always so *wobbly*. Where do you come to next?"

"You go up the steps," I continued, "and in at the door, and the very first place you come to is the Chocolate-room!"

She brightened up at this, and I heard her murmur with gusto, "Chocolate-room!"

"It's got every sort of chocolate you can think of," I went on: "soft chocolate, with sticky stuff inside, white and pink, what girls like; and hard shiny chocolate, that cracks

53

when you bite it, and takes such a nice long
time to suck!"

"I like the soft stuff best," she said: "'cos
you can eat such a lot more of it!"

This was to me a new aspect of the chocolate
question, and I regarded her with interest and
some respect. With us, chocolate was none
too common a thing, and, whenever we happened
to come by any, we resorted to the quaintest
devices in order to make it last out. Still,
legends had reached us of children who actually
had, from time to time, as much chocolate as
they could possibly eat; and here, apparently,
was one of them.

"You can have all the creams," I said mag-
nanimously, "and I'll eat the hard sticks, 'cos
I like 'em best."

"Oh, but you must n't!" she cried impetu-
ously. "You must eat the same as I do! It
is n't nice to want to eat different. I'll tell you
what — you must give *me* all the chocolate, and
then I'll give *you* — I'll give you what you
ought to have!"

"Oh, all right," I said in a subdued sort of

way. It seemed a little hard to be put under
a sentimental restriction like this in one's own
Chocolate-room.

"In the next room you come to," I proceeded,
"there's fizzy drinks! There's a marble-slab
business all round the room, and little silver
taps; and you just turn the right tap, and have
any kind of fizzy drink you want."

"What fizzy drinks are there?" she inquired.

"Oh, all sorts," I answered hastily, hurrying
on. (She might restrict my eatables, but I'd
be hanged if I was going to have her meddle
with my drinks.) "Then you go down the
corridor, and at the back of the palace there's
a great big park — the finest park you ever saw.
And there's ponies to ride on, and carriages
and carts; and a little railway, all complete,
engine and guard's van and all; and you work
it yourself, and you can go first-class, or in
the van, or on the engine, just whichever you
choose."

"I'd go on the engine," she murmured
dreamily. "No, I wouldn't, I'd — "

"Then there's all the soldiers," I struck in.

Really the line had to be drawn somewhere, and I could not have my railway system disorganised and turned upside down by a mere girl. "There's any quantity of 'em, fine big soldiers, and they all belong to me. And a row of brass cannons all along the terrace! And every now and then I give the order, and they fire off all the guns!"

"No, they don't," she interrupted hastily. "I won't have 'em fire off any guns! You must tell 'em not to. I hate guns, and as soon as they begin firing I shall run right away!"

"But — but that's what they're *there* for," I protested, aghast.

"I don't care," she insisted. "They mustn't do it. They can walk about behind me if they like, and talk to me, and carry things. But they mustn't fire off any guns."

I was sadly conscious by this time that in this brave palace of mine, wherein I was wont to swagger daily, irresponsible and unquestioned, I was rapidly becoming — so to speak — a mere lodger. The idea of my fine big soldiers being told off to "carry things"! I was not inclined to tell her any more, though there still remained plenty more to tell.

" Any other boys there?" she asked presently, in a casual sort of way.

" Oh yes," I unguardedly replied. " Nice chaps, too. We'll have great—" Then I recollected myself. " We'll play with them, of course," I went on. " But you are going to be *my* friend, are n't you? And you'll come in *my* boat, and we'll travel in the guard's van together, and I'll stop the soldiers firing off their guns!"

But she looked mischievously away, and— do what I would— I could not get her to promise.

Just then the striking of the village clock awoke within me another clamorous timepiece, reminding me of mid-day mutton a good half-mile away, and of penalties and curtailments attaching to a late appearance. We took a hurried farewell of each other, and before we parted I got from her an admission that she might be gardening again that afternoon, if only the worms would be less aggressive and give her a chance.

"Remember," I said as I turned to go, "you must n't tell anybody about what I've been telling you!"

She appeared to hesitate, swinging one leg to and fro while she regarded me sideways with half-shut eyes.

"It's a dead secret," I said artfully. "A secret between us two, and nobody knows it except ourselves!"

Then she promised, nodding violently, big-eyed, her mouth pursed up small. The delight of revelation, and the bliss of possessing a secret, run each other very close. But the latter generally wins — for a time.

I had passed the mutton stage and was weltering in warm rice pudding, before I found leisure to pause and take in things generally; and then a glance in the direction of the window told me, to my dismay, that it was raining hard. This was annoying in every way, for, even if it cleared up later, the worms — I knew well from experience — would be offensively numerous and frisky. Sulkily I said grace and accompanied the others upstairs to the schoolroom; where I got out my paint-box and resolved to devote my-self seriously to Art, which of late I had much neglected. Harold got hold of a sheet of paper and a pencil, retired to a table in the corner, squared his elbows, and protruded his tongue. Literature had always been *his* form of artistic expression.

Selina had a fit of the fidgets, bred of the unpromising weather, and, instead of settling down to something on her own account, must needs walk round and annoy us artists, intent on embodying our conceptions of the ideal. She had been looking over my shoulder some minutes before I knew of it; or I would have had a word or two to say upon the subject.

"I suppose you call that thing a ship," she remarked contemptuously. "Who ever heard of a pink ship? Hoo-hoo!"

I stifled my wrath, knowing that in order to score properly it was necessary to keep a cool head.

"There is a pink ship," I observed with forced calmness, "lying in the toy-shop window now. You can go and look at it if you like. D' you suppose you know more about ships than the fellows who make 'em?"

Selina, baffled for the moment, returned to the charge presently.

" Those are funny things, too," she observed. " S'pose they 're meant to be trees. But they 're *blue*."

" They *are* trees," I replied with severity ; " and they *are* blue. They 've *got* to be blue, 'cos you stole my gamboge last week, so I can't mix up any green."

" *Didn't* steal your gamboge," declared Selina, haughtily, edging away, however, in the direction of Harold. " And I would n't tell lies, either, if I was you, about a dirty little bit of gamboge."

I preserved a discreet silence. After all, I knew *she* knew she stole my gamboge.

The moment Harold became conscious of Selina's stealthy approach, he dropped his pencil and flung himself flat upon the table, protecting thus his literary efforts from chilling criticism by the interposed thickness of his person. From somewhere in his interior proceeded a heart-rending compound of squeal and whistle, as of escaping steam, — long-drawn, ear-piercing, unvarying in note.

"I only just want to see," protested Selina, struggling to uproot his small body from the scrawl it guarded. But Harold clung limpet-like to the table edge, and his shrill protest continued to deafen humanity and to threaten even the serenities of Olympus. The time seemed come for a demonstration in force. Personally I cared little what soul-outpourings of Harold were pirated by Selina — she was pretty sure to get hold of them sooner or later — and indeed I rather welcomed the diversion as favourable to the undisturbed pursuit of Art. But the clannishness of sex has its unwritten laws. Boys, as such, are sufficiently put upon, mal-treated, trodden under, as it is. Should they fail to hang together in perilous times, what disasters, what ignominies, may not be looked for? Possibly even an extinction of the tribe. I dropped my paint brush and sailed shouting into the fray.

The result for a short space hung dubious.

DREAM DAYS

There is a period of life when the difference of
a year or two in age far outweighs the minor
advantage of sex. Then the gathers of Selina's
frock came away with a sound like the rattle of
distant musketry; and this calamity it was,
rather than mere brute compulsion, that quelled
her indomitable spirit.

The female tongue is mightier than the sword,
as I soon had good reason to know, when Selina,
her riven garment held out at length, avenged
her discomfiture with the Greek-fire of person-
alities and abuse. Every black incident in my
short, but not stainless, career — every error,
every folly, every penalty ignobly suffered —
were paraded before me as in a magic-lantern
show. The information, however, was not particularly new to me, and the effect was staled
by previous rehearsals. Besides, a victory
remains a victory, whatever the moral character
of the triumphant general.

Harold chuckled and crowed as he dropped
from the table, revealing the document over
which so many gathers had sighed their short
lives out. "*You* can read it if you like," he

said to me gratefully. "It's only a Death-letter."

It had never been possible to say what Harold's particular amusement of the hour might turn out to be. One thing only was certain, that it would be something improbable, unguessable, not to be foretold. Who, for instance, in search of relaxation, would ever dream of choosing the drawing-up of a testamentary disposition of property? Yet this was the form taken by Harold's latest craze; and in justice this much had to be said for him, that in the christening of his amusement he had gone right to the heart of the matter. The words "will" and "testament" have various meanings and uses; but about the signification of "death-letter" there can be no manner of doubt. I smoothed out the crumpled paper and read. In actual form it deviated considerably from that usually adopted by family solicitors of standing, the only resemblance, indeed, lying in the absence of punctuation.

"my dear edward (it ran) when I die I leave all my muny to you my walkin sticks wips my crop my sord and

gun bricks forts and all things i have goodbye my dear
charlotte when i die I leave you my wach and cumpus
and pencel case my salors and camperdown my picteres
and evthing goodbye your loving brother armen my dear
Martha I love you very much i leave you my garden my
mice and rabets my plants in pots when I die please take
care of them my dear —" *Cætera desunt.*

" Why, you 're not leaving *me* anything ! "
exclaimed Selina, indignantly. " You 're a
regular mean little boy, and I 'll take back the
last birthday present I gave you ! "

" I don't care," said Harold, repossessing
himself of the document. " I *was* going to
leave you something, but I sha' n't now, 'cos
you tried to read my death-letter before I was
dead ! "

" Then I 'll write a death-letter myself,"
retorted Selina, scenting an artistic vengeance :
" and I sha' n't leave you a single thing ! " And
she went off in search of a pencil.

The tempest within-doors had kept my attention off the condition of things without. But
now a glance through the window told me that
the rain had entirely ceased, and that everything
was bathed instead in a radiant glow of sunlight,

more golden than any gamboge of mine could possibly depict. Leaving Selina and Harold to settle their feud by a mutual disinheritance, I slipped from the room and escaped into the open air, eager to pick up the loose end of my new friendship just where I had dropped it that morning. In the glorious reaction of the sunshine after the downpour, with its moist warm smells, bespanglement of greenery, and inspiriting touch of rain-washed air, the parks and palaces of the imagination glowed with a livelier iris, and their blurred beauties shone out again with fresh blush and palpitation. As I sped along to the tryst, again I accompanied my new comrade along the corridors of my pet palace into which I had so hastily introduced her ; and on reflection I began to see that it would n't work properly. I had made a mistake, and those were not the surroundings in which she was most fitted to shine. However, it really did not matter much ; I had other palaces to place at her disposal — plenty of 'em ; and on a further acquaintance with and knowledge of her tastes, no doubt I could find something to suit her.

There was a real Arabian one, for instance, which I visited but rarely — only just when I was in the fine Oriental mood for it ; a wonder of silk hangings, fountains of rosewater, pavilions, and minarets. Hundreds of silent, well-trained slaves thronged the stairs and alleys of this establishment, ready to fetch and carry for her all day, if she wished it ; and my brave soldiers would be spared the indignity. Also there were processions through the bazaar at odd moments — processions with camels, elephants, and palanquins. Yes, she was more suited for the East, this imperious young person ; and I determined that thither she should be personally conducted as soon as ever might be.

I reached the fence and climbed up two bars of it, and leaning over I looked this way and that for my twin-souled partner of the morning. It was not long before I caught sight of her, only a short distance away. Her back was towards me and — well, one can never foresee exactly how one will find things — she was talking to a Boy.

Of course there are boys and boys, and Lord knows I was never narrow. But this was the parson's son from an adjoining village, a red-headed boy and as common a little beast as ever stepped. He cultivated ferrets — his only good point ; and it was evidently through the medium of this art that he was basely supplanting me, for her head was bent absorbedly over something he carried in his hands. With some trepidation I called out, " Hi ! " But answer there was none. Then again I called, " Hi ! " but this time with a sickening sense of failure and of doom. She replied only by a complex gesture, decisive in import if not easily described. A petulant toss of the head, a jerk of the left shoulder, and a backward kick of the left foot, all delivered at once — that was all, and that was enough. The red-headed boy never even condescended to glance my way. Why, indeed, should he ? I dropped from the fence without another effort, and took my way homewards along the weary road.

Little inclination was left to me, at first, for any solitary visit to my accustomed palace, the

pleasures of which I had so recently tasted in
company ; and yet after a minute or two I found
myself, from habit, sneaking off there much as
usual.   Presently I became aware of a certain
solace and consolation in my newly-recovered
independence of action.   Quit of all female
whims and fanciful restrictions, I rowed, sailed,
or punted, just as I pleased ; in the Chocolate-
room I cracked and nibbled the hard sticks,
with a certain contempt for those who preferred
the soft, veneered article ; and I mixed and
quaffed countless fizzy drinks without dread of
any prohibitionist.   Finally, I swaggered into
the park, paraded all my soldiers on the terrace,
and, bidding them take the time from me, gave
the order to fire off all the guns.

THE MAGIC RING

"Oh, to be a splendid fellow like this, self-contained, ready of speech, agile beyond conception, braving the forces of society, his hand against everyone, and yet always getting the best of it!"

THE MAGIC RING

GROWN-UP people really ought to be more careful. Among themselves it may seem but a small thing to give their word and take back their word. For them there are so many compensations. Life lies at their feet, a party-coloured india-rubber ball; they may kick it this way or kick it that, it turns up blue, yellow, or green, but always coloured and glistening. Thus one sees it happen almost every day, and, with a jest and a laugh, the thing is over, and the disappointed one turns to fresh pleasure, lying ready to his hand. But with those who are below them, whose little globe is swayed by them, who rush to build star-pointing alhambras on their most casual word, they really ought to be more careful.

In this case of the circus, for instance, it was not as if we had led up to the subject. It was

they who began it entirely — prompted thereto
by the local newspaper. "What, a circus!"
said they, in their irritating, casual way : "that
would be nice to take the children to. Wednesday would be a good day. Suppose we go
on Wednesday. Oh, and pleats are being worn
again, with rows of deep braid," etc.

What the others thought I know not ; what
they said, if they said anything, I did not com-
prehend. For me the house was bursting, walls
seemed to cramp and to stifle, the roof was
jumping and lifting. Escape was the imperative
thing — to escape into the open air, to shake off
bricks and mortar, and to wander in the unfre-
quented places of the earth, the more properly
to take in the passion and the promise of the
giddy situation.

Nature seemed prim and staid that day, and
the globe gave no hint that it was flying round
a circus ring of its own. Could they really be
true, I wondered, all those bewildering things
I had heard tell of circuses ? Did long-tailed
ponies really walk on their hind-legs and fire
off pistols ? Was it humanly possible for clowns

to perform one-half of the bewitching drolleries recorded in history? And how, oh, how dare I venture to believe that, from off the backs of creamy Arab steeds, ladies of more than earthly beauty discharged themselves through paper hoops? No, it was not altogether possible, there must have been some exaggeration. Still, I would be content with very little, I would take a low percentage — a very small proportion of the circus myth would more than satisfy me. But again, even supposing that history were, once in a way, no liar, could it be that I myself was really fated to look upon this thing in the flesh and to live through it, to survive the rapture? No, it was altogether too much. Something was bound to happen, one of us would develop measles, the world would blow up with a loud explosion. I must not dare, I must not presume, to entertain the smallest hope. I must endeavour sternly to think of something else.

Needless to say, I thought, I dreamed of nothing else, day or night. Waking, I walked arm-in-arm with a clown, and cracked a portentous whip to the brave music of a band. Sleep-

ing, I pursued — perched astride of a coal-black
horse — a princess all gauze and spangles, who
always managed to keep just one unattainable
length ahead. In the early morning Harold
and I, once fully awake, cross-examined each
other as to the possibilities of this or that circus
tradition, and exhausted the lore long ere the
first housemaid was stirring. In this state of
exaltation we slipped onward to what promised
to be a day of all white days — which brings me
right back to my text, that grown-up people
really ought to be more careful.

I had known it could never really be ; I had
said so to myself a dozen times. The vision
was too sweetly ethereal for embodiment. Yet
the pang of the disillusionment was none the less
keen and sickening, and the pain was as that
of a corporeal wound. It seemed strange and
foreboding, when we entered the breakfast-room,
not to find everybody cracking whips, jumping
over chairs, and whooping in ecstatic rehearsal
of the wild reality to come. The situation became grim and pallid indeed, when I caught the
expressions "garden-party" and "my mauve

tulle," and realised that they both referred to that very afternoon. And every minute, as I sat silent and listened, my heart sank lower and lower, descending relentlessly like a clock-weight into my boot soles.

Throughout my agony I never dreamed of resorting to a direct question, much less a reproach. Even during the period of joyful anticipation some fear of breaking the spell had kept me from any bald circus talk in the presence of them. But Harold, who was built in quite another way, so soon as he discerned the drift of their conversation and heard the knell of all his hopes, filled the room with wail and clamour of bereavement. The grinning welkin rang with " Circus!" " Circus!" shook the window-panes; the mocking walls re-echoed " Circus!" Circus he would have, and the whole circus, and nothing but the circus. No compromise for him, no evasions, no fallacious, unsecured promises to pay. He had drawn his cheque on the Bank of Expectation, and it had got to be cashed then and there; else he would yell, and yell himself into a fit, and come out of it and yell again. Yelling should be his profession, his art, his mission, his career. He was qualified, he was resolute, and he was in no hurry to retire from the business.

The noisy ones of the world, if they do not always shout themselves into the imperial purple, are sure at least of receiving attention. If they cannot sell everything at their own price, one thing — silence — must, at any cost, be purchased of them. Harold accordingly had to be consoled by the employment of every specious fallacy and base-born trick known to those whose doom it is to handle children. For me their hollow cajolery had no interest, I could pluck no consolation out of their bankrupt though prodigal pledges. I only waited till that hateful, well-known " Some other time, dear ! " told me that hope was finally dead. Then I left the room without any remark. It made it worse — if anything could — to hear that stale, worn-out old phrase, still supposed by those dullards to have some efficacy.

To nature, as usual, I drifted by instinct, and there, out of the track of humanity, under a

friendly hedge-row had my black hour unseen.
The world was a globe no longer, space was no
more filled with whirling circuses of spheres.
That day the old beliefs rose up and asserted
themselves, and the earth was flat again — ditch-
riddled, stagnant, and deadly flat. The unde-
viating roads crawled straight and white, elms
dressed themselves stiffly along inflexible hedges,
all nature, centrifugal no longer, sprawled flatly
in lines out to its farthest edge, and I felt just
like walking out to that terminus, and dropping
quietly off. Then, as I sat there, morosely
chewing bits of stick, the recollection came
back to me of certain fascinating advertisements
I had spelled out in the papers — advertisements
of great and happy men, owning big ships of
tonnage running into four figures, who yet craved,
to the extent of public supplication, for the sympathetic co-operation of youths as apprentices.
I did not rightly know what apprentices might
be, nor whether I was yet big enough to be
styled a youth, but one thing seemed clear,
that, by some such means as this, whatever the
intervening hardships, I could eventually visit

all the circuses of the world — the circuses of merry France and gaudy Spain, of Holland and Bohemia, of China and Peru. Here was a plan worth thinking out in all its bearings ; for something had presently to be done to end this intolerable state of things.

Mid-day, and even feeding-time, passed by gloomily enough, till a small disturbance occurred which had the effect of releasing some of the electricity with which the air was charged. Harold, it should be explained, was of a very different mental mould, and never brooded, moped, nor ate his heart out over any disappointment. One wild outburst — one dissolution of a minute into his original elements of air and water, of tears and outcry — so much insulted nature claimed. Then he would pull himself together, iron out his countenance with a smile, and adjust himself to the new condition of things.

If the gods are ever grateful to man for anything, it is when he is so good as to display a short memory. The Olympians were never slow to recognise this quality of Harold's, in which,

indeed, their salvation lay, and on this occasion
their gratitude had taken the practical form of
a fine fat orange, tough-rinded as oranges of
those days were wont to be. This he had evis-
cerated in the good old-fashioned manner, by
biting out a hole in the shoulder, inserting a
lump of sugar therein, and then working it
cannily till the whole soul and body of the
orange passed glorified through the sugar into
his being. Thereupon, filled full of orange-
juice and iniquity, he conceived a deadly snare.
Having deftly patted and squeezed the orange-
skin till it resumed its original shape, he filled
it up with water, inserted a fresh lump of sugar
in the orifice, and, issuing forth, blandly proffered
it to me as I sat moodily in the doorway dream-
ing of strange wild circuses under tropic skies.

Such a stale old dodge as this would hardly
have taken me in at ordinary moments. But
Harold had reckoned rightly upon the disturbing
effect of ill-humour, and had guessed, perhaps,
that I thirsted for comfort and consolation, and
would not criticise too closely the source from
which they came. Unthinkingly I grasped the

golden fraud, which collapsed at my touch, and squirted its contents into my eyes and over my collar, till the nethermost parts of me were damp with the water that had run down my neck. In an instant I had Harold down, and, with all the energy of which I was capable, devoted myself to grinding his head into the gravel; while he, realising that the closure was applied, and that the time for discussion or argument was past, sternly concentrated his powers on kicking me in the stomach.

Some people can never allow events to work themselves out quietly. At this juncture one of Them swooped down on the scene, pouring shrill, misplaced abuse on both of us: on me for ill-treating my younger brother, whereas it was distinctly I who was the injured and the deceived; on him for the high offence of assault and battery on a clean collar — a collar which I had myself deflowered and defaced, shortly before, in sheer desperate ill-temper. Disgusted and defiant we fled in different directions, rejoining each other later in the kitchen-garden; and as we strolled along together, our short feud forgotten, Harold observed, gloomily : " I should like to be a cave-man, like Uncle George was tellin' us about : with a flint hatchet and no clothes, and live in a cave and not know anybody ! "

"And if anyone came to see us we did n't like," I joined in, catching on to the points of the idea, " we 'd hit him on the head with the hatchet till he dropped down dead."

" And then," said Harold, warming up, "we 'd drag him into the cave and *skin him !* "

For a space we gloated silently over the fair scene our imaginations had conjured up. It was *blood* we felt the need of just then. We wanted no luxuries, nothing dear-bought nor far-fetched. Just plain blood, and nothing else, and plenty of it.

Blood, however, was not to be had. The time was out of joint, and we had been born too late. So we went off to the green-house, crawled into the heating arrangement underneath, and played at the dark and dirty and unrestricted life of cave-men till we were heartily sick of it. Then we emerged once more into historic times, and went off to the road to look for something living and sentient to throw stones at.

Nature, so often a cheerful ally, sometimes sulks and refuses to play. When in this mood she passes the word to her underlings, and all the little people of fur and feather take the hint and slip home quietly by back streets. In vain we scouted, lurked, crept, and ambuscaded. Everything that usually scurried, hopped, or fluttered — the small society of the undergrowth — seemed to have engagements elsewhere. The horrid thought that perhaps they had all gone off to the circus occurred to us simultaneously, and we humped ourselves up on the fence and felt bad. Even the sound of approaching wheels failed to stir any interest in us. When you are bent on throwing stones at something, humanity seems obtrusive and better away. Then suddenly we both jumped off the fence together, our faces clearing. For our educated ear had told us that the approaching rattle could only proceed from a dog-cart, and we felt sure it must be the funny man.

THE MAGIC RING

We called him the funny man because he was sad and serious, and said little, but gazed right into our souls, and made us tell him just what was on our minds at the time, and then came out with some magnificently luminous suggestion that cleared every cloud away. What was more, he would then go off with us at once and play the thing right out to its finish, earnestly and devotedly, putting all other things aside. So we called him the funny man, meaning only that he was different from those others who thought it incumbent on them to play the painful mummer. The ideal as opposed to the real man was what we meant, only we were not acquainted with the phrase. Those others, with their laboured jests and clumsy contortions, doubtless flattered themselves that *they* were funny men; we, who had to sit through and applaud the painful performance, knew better.

He pulled up to a walk as soon as he caught sight of us, and the dog-cart crawled slowly along till it stopped just opposite. Then he leant his chin on his hand and regarded us long and soulfully, yet said he never a word; while we jigged up and down in the dust, grinning bashfully but with expectation. For you never knew exactly what this man might say or do.

" You look bored," he remarked presently; "thoroughly bored. Or else — let me see; you 're not married, are you?"

He asked this in such sad earnestness that we hastened to assure him we were not married, though we felt he ought to have known that much; we had been intimate for some time.

" Then it 's only boredom," he said. " Just satiety and world-weariness. Well, if you assure me you are n't married you can climb into this cart and I 'll take you for a drive. I 'm bored, too. I want to do something dark and dreadful and exciting."

We clambered in, of course, yapping with delight and treading all over his toes; and as we set off, Harold demanded of him imperiously whither he was going.

" My wife," he replied, " has ordered me to go and look up the curate and bring him home to tea. Does that sound sufficiently exciting for you?"

Our faces fell. The curate of the hour was not a success, from our point of view. He was not a funny man, in any sense of the word.

" — but I 'm not going to," he added, cheerfully. "Then I was to stop at some cottage and ask — what was it? There was *nettle-rash* mixed up in it, I 'm sure. But never mind, I 've forgotten, and it does n't matter. Look here, we 're three desperate young fellows who stick at nothing. Suppose we go off to the circus?"

Of certain supreme moments it is not easy to write. The varying shades and currents of emotion may indeed be put into words by those specially skilled that way; they often are, at considerable length. But the sheer, crude article itself — the strong, live thing that leaps up inside you and swells and strangles you, the dizziness of revulsion that takes the breath like cold water — who shall depict this and live? All I knew was that I would have died then and there, cheerfully, for the funny man; that I longed for red Indians to spring out from the hedge on the dog-cart, just to show what I would do; and that, with all this, I could not find the least little word to say to him.

Harold was less taciturn. With shrill voice, uplifted in solemn chant, he sang the great spheral circus song, and the undying glory of the Ring. Of its timeless beginning he sang, of its fashioning by cosmic forces, and of its harmony with the stellar plan. Of horses he sang, of their strength, their swiftness, and their docility as to tricks. Of clowns again, of the glory of knavery, and of the eternal type that shall endure. Lastly he sang of Her — the Woman of the Ring — flawless, complete, untrammelled in each subtly curving limb; earth's highest output, time's noblest expression. At least, he doubtless sang all these things and more — he certainly seemed to; though all that was distinguishable was, "We're-goin'-to-the-circus!" and then, once more, "We're-goin'-to-the-circus!" — the sweet rhythmic phrase repeated again and again. But indeed I cannot be quite sure, for I heard confusedly, as in a dream. Wings of fire sprang from the old mare's shoulders. We whirled on our way

through purple clouds, and earth and the rattle
of wheels were far away below.

The dream and the dizziness were still in my
head when I found myself, scarce conscious of
intermediate steps, seated actually in the circus
at last, and took in the first sniff of that intoxicating circus smell that will stay by me while
this clay endures. The place was beset by a
hum and a glitter and a mist ; suspense brooded
large o'er the blank, mysterious arena. Strung
up to the highest pitch of expectation, we knew
not from what quarter, in what divine shape, the
first surprise would come.

A thud of unseen hoofs first set us a-quiver ;
then a crash of cymbals, a jangle of bells, a
hoarse applauding roar, and Coralie was in the
midst of us, whirling past 'twixt earth and sky,
now erect, flushed, radiant, now crouched to the
flowing mane ; swung and tossed and moulded
by the maddening dance-music of the band.
The mighty whip of the count in the frock-coat
marked time with pistol-shots ; his war-cry,
whooping clear above the music, fired the blood
with a passion for splendid deeds, as Coralie,

laughing, exultant, crashed through the paper hoops. We gripped the red cloth in front of us, and our souls sped round and round with Coralie, leaping with her, prone with her, swung by mane or tail with her. It was not only the ravishment of her delirious feats, nor her cream-coloured horse of fairy breed, long-tailed, roe-footed, an enchanted prince surely, if ever there was one! It was her more than mortal beauty — displayed, too, under conditions never vouchsafed to us before — that held us spell-bound. What princess had arms so dazzlingly white, or went delicately clothed in such pink and spangles? Hitherto we had known the outward woman as but a drab thing, hour-glass shaped, nearly legless, bunched here, constricted there, slow of movement, and given to deprecating lusty action of limb. Here was a revelation! From henceforth our imaginations would have to be revised and corrected up to date. In one of those swift rushes the mind makes in high-strung moments, I saw myself and Coralie, close enfolded, pacing the world together, o'er hill and plain, through storied cities, past rows of applauding relations, —

THE MAGIC RING

I in my Sunday knickerbockers, she in her pink and spangles.

Summers sicken, flowers fail and die, all beauty but rides round the ring and out at the portal; even so Coralie passed in her turn, poised sideways, panting, on her steed; lightly swayed as a tulip-bloom, bowing on this side and on that as she disappeared; and with her went my heart and my soul, and all the light and the glory and the entrancement of the scene.

Harold woke up with a gasp. "Wasn't she beautiful?" he said, in quite a subdued way for him. I felt a momentary pang. We had been friendly rivals before, in many an exploit; but here was altogether a more serious affair. Was this, then, to be the beginning of strife and coldness, of civil war on the hearthstone and the sundering of old ties? Then I recollected the true position of things, and felt very sorry for Harold; for it was inexorably written that he would have to give way to me, since I was the elder. Rules were not made for nothing, in a sensibly constructed universe.

There was little more to wait for, now Coralie

had gone; yet I lingered still, on the chance of
her appearing again. Next moment the clown
tripped up and fell flat, with magnificent artifice,
and at once fresh emotions began to stir. Love
had endured its little hour, and stern ambition
now asserted itself. Oh, to be a splendid fellow
like this, self-contained, ready of speech, agile
beyond conception, braving the forces of society,
his hand against everyone, yet always getting
the best of it! What freshness of humour, what
courtesy to dames, what triumphant ability to
discomfit rivals, frock-coated and moustached
though they might be! And what a grand,
self-confident straddle of the legs! Who could
desire a finer career than to go through life thus
gorgeously equipped! Success was his key-
note, adroitness his panoply, and the mellow
music of laughter his instant reward. Even
Coralie's image wavered and receded. I would
come back to her in the evening, of course; but
I would be a clown all the working hours of
the day.

The short interval was ended: the band, with
long-drawn chords, sounded a prelude touched

with significance; and the programme, in letters overtopping their fellows, proclaimed Zephyrine, the Bride of the Desert, in her unequalled bareback equestrian interlude. So sated was I already with beauty and with wit, that I hardly dared hope for a fresh emotion. Yet her title was tinged with romance, and Coralie's display had aroused in me an interest in her sex which even herself had failed to satisfy entirely.

Brayed in by trumpets, Zephyrine swung passionately into the arena. With a bound she stood erect, one foot upon each of her supple, plunging Arabs, and at once I knew that my fate was sealed, my chapter closed, and the Bride of the Desert was the one bride for me. Black was her raiment, great silver stars shone through it, caught in the dusky twilight of her gauze; black as her own hair were the two mighty steeds she bestrode. In a tempest they thundered by, in a whirlwind, a *scirocco* of tan; her cheeks bore the kiss of an Eastern sun, and the sand-storms of her native desert were her satellites. What was Coralie, with her pink silk, her golden hair and slender limbs, beside this magnificent, full-figured Cleopatra? In a twinkling we were scouring the desert — she and I and the two coal-black horses. Side by side, keeping pace in our swinging gallop, we distanced the ostrich, we outstrode the zebra; and, as we went, it seemed the wilderness blossomed like the rose.

. . . .

I know not rightly how we got home that evening. On the road there were everywhere strange presences, and the thud of phantom hoofs encircled us. In my nose was the pungent circus-smell; the crack of the whip and the frank laugh of the clown were in my ears. The funny man thoughtfully abstained from conversation, and left our illusion quite alone, sparing us all jarring criticism and analysis; and he gave me no chance, when he deposited us at our gate, to get rid of the clumsy expressions of gratitude I had been laboriously framing. For the rest of the evening, distraught and silent, I only heard the march-music of the band, playing on in some corner of my brain. When at last my head touched the pillow, in

THE MAGIC RING

a trice I was with Zephyrine, riding the bound-
less Sahara, cheek to cheek, the world well
lost ; while at times, through the sand-clouds
that encircled us, glimmered the eyes of Coralie,
touched, one fancied, with something of a tender
reproach.

ITS WALLS WERE AS OF JASPER

"While every plunge of our bows brought us nearer to the
happy island."

ITS WALLS WERE AS OF JASPER

IN the long winter evenings, when we had the
picture-books out on the floor, and sprawled
together over them with elbows deep in the
hearth-rug, the first business to be gone through
was the process of allotment. All the characters in the pictures had to be assigned and dealt
out among us, according to seniority, as far as
they would go. When once that had been sat-
isfactorily completed, the story was allowed to
proceed ; and thereafter, in addition to the excitement of the plot, one always possessed a
personal interest in some particular member of
the cast, whose successes or rebuffs one took
as so much private gain or loss.

For Edward this was satisfactory enough.
Claiming his right of the eldest, he would annex
the hero in the very frontispiece ; and for the
rest of the story his career, if chequered at

intervals, was sure of heroic episodes and a glorious close. But his juniors, who had to put up with characters of a clay more mixed — nay, sometimes with undiluted villany — were hard put to it on occasion to defend their other selves (as it was strict etiquette to do) from ignominy perhaps only too justly merited.

Edward was indeed a hopeless grabber. In the "Buffalo-book," for instance (so named from the subject of its principal picture, though indeed it dealt with varied slaughter in every zone), Edward was the stalwart, bearded figure, with yellow leggings and a powder-horn, who undauntedly discharged the fatal bullet into the shoulder of the great bull bison, charging home to within a yard of his muzzle. To me was allotted the subsidiary character of the friend who had succeeded in bringing down a cow; while Harold had to be content to hold Edward's spare rifle in the background, with evident signs of uneasiness. Farther on, again, where the magnificent chamois sprang rigid into mid-air, Edward, crouched dizzily against the precipice-face, was the sportsman from whose weapon a puff of white smoke was floating away. A bare-kneed guide was all that fell to my share, while poor Harold had to take the boy with the haversack, or abandon, for this occasion at least, all Alpine ambitions.

Of course the girls fared badly in this book, and it was not surprising that they preferred the " Pilgrim's Progress " (for instance), where women had a fair show, and there was generally enough of 'em to go round; or a good fairy story, wherein princesses met with a healthy appreciation. But indeed we were all best pleased with a picture wherein the characters just fitted us, in number, sex, and qualifications; and this, to us, stood for artistic merit.

All the Christmas numbers, in their gilt frames on the nursery-wall, had been gone through and allotted long ago; and in these, sooner or later, each one of us got a chance to figure in some satisfactory and brightly coloured situation. Few of the other pictures about the house afforded equal facilities. They were generally wanting in figures, and even when these were present they lacked dramatic interest. In this picture that I have to speak about, although the characters had a stupid way of not doing anything, and apparently not wanting to do anything, there was at least a sufficiency of them; so in due course they were allotted, too.

In itself the picture, which — in its ebony and tortoise-shell frame — hung in a corner of the dining-room, had hitherto possessed no special interest for us, and would probably never have been dealt with at all but for a revolt of the girls against a succession of books on sport, in which the illustrator seemed to have forgotten that there were such things as women in the world. Selina accordingly made for it one rainy morning, and announced that she was the lady seated in the centre, whose gown of rich, flowered brocade fell in such straight, severe lines to her feet, whose cloak of dark blue was held by a jewelled clasp, and whose long, fair hair was crowned with a diadem of gold and pearl. Well, we had no objection to that; it seemed fair enough, especially to Edward, who promptly proceeded to "grab" the armour-man who stood leaning on his shield at the lady's right hand. A dainty and delicate armour-man this! And I confess, though I knew it was all right and fair and orderly, I felt a slight pang when he passed out of my reach into Edward's possession. His armour was just the sort I wanted myself — scalloped and fluted and shimmering and spotless; and, though he was but a boy by his beardless face and golden hair, the shattered spear-shaft in his grasp proclaimed him a genuine fighter and fresh from some such agreeable work. Yes, I grudged Edward the armour-man, and when he said I could have the fellow on the other side, I hung back and said I'd think about it.

This fellow had no armour nor weapons, but wore a plain jerkin with a leather pouch — a mere civilian — and with one hand he pointed to a wound in his thigh. I didn't care about him, and when Harold eagerly put in his claim I gave way and let him have the man. The cause of Harold's anxiety only came out later. It was the wound he coveted, it seemed. He wanted to have a big, sore wound of his very own, and go about and show it to people, and excite their envy or win their respect. Charlotte was only too pleased to take the child-angel seated at the lady's feet, grappling with a musical instrument much too big for her. Charlotte wanted wings badly, and, next to those, a guitar or a banjo. The angel, besides, wore an amber necklace, which took her fancy immensely.

This left the picture allotted, with the exception of two or three more angels, who peeped or perched behind the main figures with a certain subdued drollery in their faces, as if the thing had gone on long enough, and it was now time to upset something or kick up a row of some sort. We knew these good folk to be saints and angels, because we had been told they were; otherwise we should never have guessed it. Angels, as we knew them in our Sunday books, were vapid, colourless, uninteresting characters, with straight up-and-down sort of figures, white nightgowns, white wings, and the same straight yellow hair parted in the middle. They were serious, even melancholy; and we had no desire to have any traffic with them. These bright bejewelled little persons, however, piquant of face and radiant of feather, were evidently hatched from quite a different egg, and we felt we might have interests in common with them. Short-nosed, shock-headed, with mouths that went up at the corners and with an evident disregard for all their fine clothes, they would be the best of good company, we felt sure, if only we could manage to get at them. One doubt alone disturbed my mind. In games requiring agility, those wings of theirs would give them a tremendous pull. Could they be trusted to play fair? I asked Selina, who replied scornfully that angels *always* played fair. But I went back and had another look at the brown-faced one peeping over the back of the lady's chair, and still I had my doubts.

When Edward went off to school a great deal of adjustment and re-allotment took place, and all the heroes of illustrated literature were at my call, did I choose to possess them. In this particular case, however, I made no haste to seize upon the armour-man. Perhaps it was because I wanted a *fresh* saint of my own, not a stale saint that Edward had been for so long

a time. Perhaps it was rather that, ever since
I had elected to be saintless, I had got into the
habit of strolling off into the background, and
amusing myself with what I found there.

A very fascinating background it was, and
held a great deal, though so tiny. Meadow-
land came first, set with flowers, blue and red,
like gems. Then a white road ran, with wilful,
uncalled-for loops, up a steep, conical hill,
crowned with towers, bastioned walls, and bel-
fries ; and down the road the little knights came
riding, two and two. The hill on one side descended to water, tranquil, far-reaching, and
blue ; and a very curly ship lay at anchor, with
one mast having an odd sort of crow's-nest at
the top of it.

There was plenty to do in this pleasant land.
The annoying thing about it was, one could
never penetrate beyond a certain point. I might
wander up that road as often as I liked, I was
bound to be brought up at the gateway, the
funny galleried, top-heavy gateway, of the little
walled town. Inside, doubtless, there were high
jinks going on ; but the password was denied to

me. I could get on board a boat and row up
as far as the curly ship, but around the headland I might not go. On the other side, of a
surety, the shipping lay thick. The merchants
walked on the quay, and the sailors sang as they
swung out the corded bales. But as for me, I
must stay down in the meadow, and imagine it
all as best I could.

Once I broached the subject to Charlotte,
and found, to my surprise, that she had had the
same joys and encountered the same disappoint-
ments in this delectable country. She, too,
had walked up that road and flattened her nose
against that portcullis; and she pointed out
something that I had overlooked — to wit, that
if you rowed off in a boat to the curly ship, and
got hold of a rope, and clambered aboard of her,
and swarmed up the mast, and got into the
crow's-nest, you could just see over the headland, and take in at your ease the life and bustle
of the port. She proceeded to describe all the
fun that was going on there, at such length and
with so much particularity that I looked at her
suspiciously. " Why, you talk as if you 'd been

in that crow's-nest yourself!" I said. Charlotte answered nothing, but pursed her mouth up and nodded violently for some minutes; and I could get nothing more out of her. I felt rather hurt. Evidently she had managed, somehow or other, to get up into that crow's-nest. Charlotte had got ahead of me on this occasion.

It was necessary, no doubt, that grown-up people should dress themselves up and go forth to pay calls. I don't mean that we saw any sense in the practice. It would have been so much more reasonable to stay at home in your old clothes and play. But we recognised that these folk had to do many unaccountable things, and after all it was *their* life, and not ours, and we were not in a position to criticise. Besides, they had many habits more objectionable than this one, which to us generally meant a free and untrammelled afternoon, wherein to play the devil in our own way. The case was different, however, when the press-gang was abroad, when prayers and excuses were alike disregarded, and we were forced into the service, like native levies impelled toward the foe less by the inherent righteousness of the cause than by the indisputable rifles of their white allies. This was unpardonable and altogether detestable. Still, the thing happened, now and again; and when it did, there was no arguing about it. The order was for the front, and we just had to shut up and march.

Selina, to be sure, had a sneaking fondness for dressing up and paying calls, though she pretended to dislike it, just to keep on the soft side of public opinion. So I thought it extremely mean in her to have the earache on that particular afternoon when Aunt Eliza ordered the pony-carriage and went on the war-path. I was ordered also, in the same breath as the pony-carriage; and, as we eventually trundled off, it seemed to me that the utter waste of that afternoon, for which I had planned so much, could never be made up nor atoned for in all the tremendous stretch of years that still lay before me.

The house that we were bound for on this occasion was a "big house;" a generic title applied by us to the class of residence that had a long carriage-drive through rhododendrons; and a portico propped by fluted pillars; and a grave butler who bolted back swing-doors, and came down steps, and pretended to have entirely forgotten his familiar intercourse with you at less serious moments; and a big hall, where no boots or shoes or upper garments were allowed to lie about frankly and easily, as with us; and where, finally, people were apt to sit about dressed up as if they were going on to a party.

The lady who received us was effusive to Aunt Eliza and hollowly gracious to me. In ten seconds they had their heads together and were hard at it talking *clothes.* I was left high and dry on a straight-backed chair, longing to kick the legs of it, yet not daring. For a time I was content to stare; there was lots to stare at, high and low and around. Then the inevitable fidgets came on, and scratching one's legs mitigated slightly, but did not entirely disperse them. My two warders were still deep in clothes; I slipped off my chair and edged cautiously around the room, exploring, examining, recording.

ITS WALLS WERE AS OF JASPER

Many strange, fine things lay along my route — pictures and gimcracks on the walls, trinkets and globular old watches and snuff-boxes on the tables ; and I took good care to finger everything within reach thoroughly and conscientiously. Some articles, in addition, I smelt. At last in my orbit I happened on an open door, half concealed by the folds of a curtain. I glanced carefully around. They were still deep in clothes, both talking together, and I slipped through.

This was altogether a more sensible sort of room that I had got into ; for the walls were honestly upholstered with books, though these for the most part glimmered provokingly through the glass doors of their tall cases. I read their titles longingly, breathing on every accessible pane of glass, for I dared not attempt to open the doors, with the enemy encamped so near. In the window, though, on a high sort of desk, there lay, all by itself, a most promising-looking book, gorgeously bound. I raised the leaves by one corner, and like scent from a pot-pourri jar there floated out a brief vision of blues and reds, telling of pictures, and pictures all highly coloured! Here was the right sort of thing at last, and my afternoon would not be entirely wasted. I inclined an ear to the door by which I had entered. Like the brimming tide of a full-fed river the grand, eternal, inexhaustible clothes-problem bubbled and eddied and surged along. It seemed safe enough. I slid the book off its desk with some difficulty, for it was very fine and large, and staggered with it to the hearthrug — the only fit and proper place for books of quality, such as this.

They were excellent hearthrugs in that house; soft and wide, with the thickest of pile, and one's knees sank into them most comfortably. When I got the book open there was a difficulty at first in making the great stiff pages lie down. Most fortunately the coal-scuttle was actually at my elbow, and it was easy to find a flat bit of coal to lay on the refractory page. Really, it was just as if everything had been arranged for me. This was not such a bad sort of house after all.

The beginnings of the thing were gay borders

—scrolls and strap-work and diapered back-
grounds, a maze of colour, with small misshapen
figures clambering cheerily up and down everywhere. But first I eagerly scanned what text
there was in the middle, in order to get a hint
of what it was all about. Of course I was not
going to waste any time in reading. A clue,
a sign-board, a finger-post was all I required.
To my dismay and disgust it was all in a stupid
foreign language! Really, the perversity of some
people made one at times almost despair of the
whole race. However, the pictures remained;
pictures never lied, never shuffled nor evaded;
and as for the story, I could invent it myself.

Over the page I went, shifting the bit of coal
to a new position; and, as the scheme of the
picture disengaged itself from out the medley
of colour that met my delighted eyes, first there
was a warm sense of familiarity, then a dawning
recognition, and then — O then! along with
blissful certainty came the imperious need to
clasp my stomach with both hands, in order to
repress the shout of rapture that struggled to escape — it was my own little city!

I knew it well enough, I recognised it at once,
though I had never been quite so near it before.
Here was the familiar gateway, to the left that
strange, slender tower with its grim, square
head shot far above the walls; to the right,
outside the town, the hill — as of old — broke
steeply down to the sea. But to-day everything
was bigger and fresher and clearer, the walls
seemed newly hewn, gay carpets were hung out
over them, fair ladies and long-haired children
peeped and crowded on the battlements. Better
still, the portcullis was up — I could even catch
a glimpse of the sunlit square within — and a
dainty company was trooping through the gate
on horseback, two and two. Their horses, in
trappings that swept the ground, were gay as
themselves; and *they* were the gayest crew, for
dress and bearing, I had ever yet beheld. It
could mean nothing else but a wedding, I thought,
this holiday attire, this festal and solemn entry;
and, wedding or whatever it was, I meant to be
there. This time I would not be balked by any
grim portcullis; this time I would slip in with
the rest of the crowd, find out just what my little

town was like, within those exasperating walls
that had so long confronted me, and, moreover,
have my share of the fun that was evidently
going on inside. Confident, yet breathless with
expectation, I turned the page.

Joy! At last I was in it, at last I was on
the right side of those provoking walls; and,
needless to say, I looked about me with much
curiosity. A public place, clearly, though not
such as I was used to. The houses at the back
stood on a sort of colonnade, beneath which the
people jostled and crowded. The upper stories
were all painted with wonderful pictures. Above
the straight line of the roofs the deep blue of a
cloudless sky stretched from side to side. Lords
and ladies thronged the foreground, while on a
dais in the centre a gallant gentleman, just
alighted off his horse, stooped to the fingers of
a girl as bravely dressed out as Selina's lady
between the saints; and round about stood ven-
erable personages, robed in the most variegated
clothing. There were boys, too, in plenty, with
tiny red caps on their thick hair; and their shirts
had bunched up and worked out at the waist,

just as my own did so often, after chasing anybody ; and each boy of them wore an odd pair
of stockings, one blue and the other red. This
system of attire went straight to my heart. I
had tried the same thing so often, and had met
with so much discouragement ; and here, at last,
was my justification, painted deliberately in a
grown-up book ! I looked about for my saint-
friends — the armour-man and the other fellow
— but they were not to be seen. Evidently
they were unable to get off duty, even for a
wedding, and still stood on guard in that green
meadow down below. I was disappointed, too,
that not an angel was visible. One or two of
them, surely, could easily have been spared for
an hour, to run up and see the show ; and they
would have been thoroughly at home here, in
the midst of all the colour and the movement
and the fun.

But it was time to get on, for clearly the
interest was only just beginning. Over went
the next page, and there we were, the whole
crowd of us, assembled in a noble church. It
was not easy to make out exactly what was

going on; but in the throng I was delighted to
recognise my angels at last, happy and very
much at home. They had managed to get
leave off, evidently, and must have run up the
hill and scampered breathlessly through the
gate; and perhaps they cried a little when they
found the square empty, and thought the fun
must be all over. Two of them had got hold
of a great wax candle apiece, as much as they
could stagger under, and were tittering sideways
at each other as the grease ran bountifully over
their clothes. A third had strolled in among
the company, and was chatting to a young gentleman, with whom she appeared to be on the
best of terms. Decidedly, this was the right
breed of angel for us. None of your sick-bed
or night-nursery business for them!

Well, no doubt they were now being married,
He and She, just as always happened. And
then, of course, they were going to live happily
ever after; and *that* was the part I wanted to
get to. Story-books were so stupid, always
stopping at the point where they became really
nice; but this picture-story was only in its first

chapters, and at last I was to have a chance of knowing *how* people lived happily ever after. We would all go home together, He and She, and the angels, and I ; and the armour-man would be invited to come and stay. And then the story would really begin, at the point where those other ones always left off. I turned the page, and found myself free of the dim and splendid church and once more in the open country.

This was all right ; this was just as it should be. The sky was a fleckless blue, the flags danced in the breeze, and our merry bridal party, with jest and laughter, jogged down to the water-side. I was through the town by this time, and out on the other side of the hill, where I had always wanted to be ; and, sure enough, there was the harbour, all thick with curly ships. Most of them were piled high with wedding-presents — bales of silk, and gold and silver plate, and comfortable-looking bags suggesting bullion ; and the gayest ship of all lay close up to the carpeted landing-stage. Already the bride was stepping daintily down the gangway, her ladies following primly, one by one ; a few minutes more and we should all be aboard, the hawsers would splash in the water, the sails would fill and strain. From the deck I should see the little walled town recede and sink and grow dim, while every plunge of our bows brought us nearer to the happy island — it was an island we were bound for, I knew well! Already I could see the island-people waving hands on the crowded quay, whence the little houses ran up the hill to the castle, crowning all with its towers and battlements. Once more we should ride together, a merry procession, clattering up the steep street and through the grim gateway ; and then we should have arrived, then we should all dine together, then we should have reached home ! And then —

Ow! Ow! Ow!

Bitter it is to stumble out of an opalescent dream into the cold daylight ; cruel to lose in a second a sea-voyage, an island, and a castle that was to be practically your own ; but cruellest and bitterest of all to know, in addition to your loss, that the fingers of an angry aunt have you tight by the scruff of your neck. My beau-

tiful book was gone too — ravished from my
grasp by the dressy lady, who joined in the outburst of denunciation as heartily as if she had
been a relative — and naught was left me but
to blubber dismally, awakened of a sudden to
the harshness of real things and the unnumbered
hostilities of the actual world. I cared little
for their reproaches, their abuse ; but I sorrowed
heartily for my lost ship, my vanished island, my
uneaten dinner, and for the knowledge that, if
I wanted any angels to play with, I must henceforth put up with the anæmic, night-gowned
nonentities that hovered over the bed of the
Sunday-school child in the pages of the *Sabbath
Improver.*

I was led ignominiously out of the house, in a
pulpy, watery state, while the butler handled
his swing doors with a stony, impassive countenance, intended for the deception of the very
elect, though it did not deceive me. I knew
well enough that next time he was off duty, and
strolled around our way, we should meet in our
kitchen as man to man, and I would punch him
and ask him riddles, and he would teach me tricks

with corks and bits of string. So his unsympathetic manner did not add to my depression.

I maintained a diplomatic blubber long after we had been packed into our pony-carriage and the lodge-gate had clicked behind us, because it served as a sort of armour-plating against heckling and argument and abuse, and I was thinking hard and wanted to be let alone. And the thoughts that I was thinking were two.

First I thought, "I've got ahead of Charlotte *this* time!"

And next I thought, "When I've grown up big, and have money of my own, and a full-sized walking-stick, I will set out early one morning, and never stop till I get to that little walled town." There ought to be no real difficulty in the task. It only meant asking here and asking there, and people were very obliging, and I could describe every stick and stone of it.

As for the island which I had never even seen, that was not so easy. Yet I felt confident that somehow, at some time, sooner or later, I was destined to arrive.

A SAGA OF THE SEAS

"All serious resistance came to an end as soon as I had
reached the quarter-deck and cut down the pirate chief."

A SAGA OF THE SEAS

IT happened one day that some ladies came
to call, who were not at all the sort I was
used to. They suffered from a grievance, so far
as I could gather, and the burden of their plaint
was Man — Men in general and Man in particular. (Though the words were but spoken, I
could clearly discern the capital M in their acid
utterance.)

Of course I was not present officially, so to
speak. Down below, in my sub-world of chair-
legs and hearthrugs and the undersides of sofas,
I was working out my own floor-problems, while
they babbled on far above my head, considering
me as but a chair-leg, or even something lower
in the scale. Yet I was listening hard all the
time, with that respectful consideration one gives
to all grown-up people's remarks, so long as
one knows no better.

It seemed a serious indictment enough, as they rolled it out. In tact, considerateness, and right appreciation, as well as in taste and æsthetic sensibilities — we failed at every point, we breeched and bearded prentice-jobs of Nature; and I began to feel like collapsing on the carpet from sheer spiritual anæmia. But when one of them, with a swing of her skirt, prostrated a whole regiment of my brave tin soldiers, and never apologised nor even offered her aid toward revivifying the battle-line, I could not help feeling that in tactfulness and consideration for others she was still a little to seek. And I said as much, with some directness of language.

That was the end of me, from a society point of view. Rudeness to visitors was the unpardonable sin, and in two seconds I had my marching orders, and was sullenly wending my way to the St. Helena of the nursery. As I climbed the stair, my thoughts reverted somehow to a game we had been playing that very morning. It was the good old game of Rafts, — a game that will be played till all the oceans are dry and all the trees in the world are felled — and after. And we were all crowded together on the precarious little platform, and Selina occupied every bit as much room as I did, and Charlotte's legs did n't dangle over any more than Harold's. The pitiless sun overhead beat on us all with tropic impartiality, and the hungry sharks, whose fins scored the limitless Pacific stretching out on every side, were impelled by an appetite that made no exceptions as to sex. When we shared the ultimate biscuit and circulated the last water-keg, the girls got an absolute fourth apiece, and neither more nor less; and the only partiality shown was entirely in favour of Charlotte, who was allowed to perceive and to hail the saviour-sail on the horizon. And this was only because it was her turn to do so, not because she happened to be this or that. Surely, the rules .of the raft were the rules of life, and in what, then, did these visitor-ladies' grievance consist?

Puzzled and a little sulky, I pushed open the door of the deserted nursery, where the raft that had rocked beneath so many hopes and fears still occupied the ocean-floor. To the dull eye, that merely tarries upon the outsides of things, it might have appeared unromantic and even unraftlike, consisting only as it did of a round sponge-bath on a bald deal towel-horse placed flat on the floor. Even to myself much of the recent raft-glamour seemed to have departed as I half-mechanically stepped inside and curled myself up in it for a solitary voyage. Once I was in, however, the old magic and mystery returned in full flood, when I discovered that the inequalities of the towel-horse caused the bath to rock, slightly, indeed, but easily and incessantly. A few minutes of this delightful motion, and one was fairly launched. So those women below did n't want us? Well, there were other women, and other places, that did. And this was going to be no scrambling raft-affair, but a full-blooded voyage of the Man, equipped and purposeful, in search of what was his rightful own.

Whither should I shape my course, and what sort of vessel should I charter for the voyage? The shipping of all England was mine to pick from, and the far corners of the globe were my rightful inheritance. A frigate, of course, seemed the natural vehicle for a boy of spirit to set out in. And yet there was something rather " uppish " in commanding a frigate at the very first set-off, and little spread was left for the ambition. Frigates, too, could always be acquired later by sheer adventure ; and your real hero generally saved up a square-rigged ship for the final achievement and the rapt return. No, it was a schooner that I was aboard of — a schooner whose masts raked devilishly as the leaping seas hissed along her low black gunwale. Many hairbrained youths started out on a mere cutter ; but I was prudent, and besides I had some inkling of the serious affairs that were ahead.

I have said I was already on board ; and, indeed, on this occasion I was too hungry for adventure to linger over what would have been a special delight at a period of more leisure — the dangling about the harbour, the choosing your craft, selecting your shipmates, stowing your cargo, and fitting up your private cabin with everything you might want to put your hand on in any emergency whatever. I could not wait for that. Out beyond soundings the big seas were racing westward and calling me, albatrosses hovered motionless, expectant of a comrade, and a thousand islands held each of them a fresh adventure, stored up, hidden away, awaiting production, expressly saved for me. We were humming, close-hauled, down the Channel, spray in the eyes and the shrouds thrilling musically, in much less time than the average man would have taken to transfer his Gladstone bag and his rugs from the train to a sheltered place on the promenade-deck of the tame daily steamer.

So long as we were in pilotage I stuck manfully to the wheel. The undertaking was mine, and with it all its responsibilities, and there was some tricky steering to be done as we sped by headland and bay, ere we breasted the great seas outside and the land fell away behind us. But as soon as the Atlantic had opened out I began to feel that it would be rather nice to take tea by myself in my own cabin, and it therefore became necessary to invent a comrade or two, to take their turn at the wheel.

This was easy enough. A friend or two of my own age, from among the boys I knew; a friend or two from characters in the books I knew; and a friend or two from No-man's-land, where every fellow's a born sailor; and the crew was complete. I addressed them on the poop, divided them into watches, gave instructions I should be summoned on the first sign of pirates, whales, or Frenchmen, and retired below to a well-earned spell of relaxation.

That was the right sort of cabin that I stepped into, shutting the door behind me with a click. Of course, fire-arms were the first thing I looked for, and there they were, sure enough, in their racks, dozens of 'em — double-barrelled guns, and repeating-rifles, and long pistols, and shiny plated revolvers. I rang up the steward and ordered tea, with scones, and jam in its native pots — none of your finicking shallow glass dishes; and, when properly streaked with jam, and blown out with tea, I went through the armoury, clicked the rifles and revolvers, tested the edges of the cutlasses with my thumb, and filled the cartridge-belts chock-full. Everything was there, and of the best quality, just as if I had spent a whole fortnight knocking about Plymouth and ordering things. Clearly, if this cruise came to grief, it would not be for want of equipment.

Just as I was beginning on the lockers and the drawers, the watch reported icebergs on both bows — and, what was more to the point, coveys of Polar bears on the icebergs. I grasped a rifle or two, and hastened on deck. The spectacle was indeed magnificent — it generally is, with icebergs on both bows, and these were exceptionally enormous icebergs. But I had n't come there to paint Academy pictures, so the captain's gig was in the water and manned almost ere the boatswain's whistle had ceased sounding, and we were pulling hard for the Polar bears — myself and the rifles in the stern-sheets.

I have rarely enjoyed better shooting than I got during that afternoon's tramp over the icebergs. Perhaps I was in specially good form; perhaps the bears "rose" well. Anyhow, the bag was a portentous one. In later days, on reading of the growing scarcity of Polar bears, my conscience has pricked me ; but that afternoon I experienced no compunction. Nevertheless, when the huge pile of skins had been hoisted on board, and a stiff grog had been served out to the crew of the captain's gig, I ordered the schooner's head to be set due south. For icebergs were played out, for the moment, and it was getting to be time for something more tropical.

Tropical was a mild expression of what was to come, as was shortly proved. It was about three bells in the next day's forenoon watch when the look-out man first sighted the pirate brigantine. I disliked the looks of her from the first, and, after piping all hands to quarters, had the brass carronade on the fore-deck crammed with grape to the muzzle.

This proved a wise precaution. For the flagitious pirate craft, having crept up to us under the colours of the Swiss Republic, a state with which we were just then on the best possible terms, suddenly shook out the skull-and-cross-bones at her mast-head, and let fly with round-shot at close quarters, knocking into pieces several of my crew, who could ill be spared. The sight of their disconnected limbs aroused my ire to its utmost height, and I let them have the contents of the brass carronade, with ghastly effect. Next moment the hulls of the two ships were grinding together, the cold steel flashed from its scabbard, and the death-grapple had begun.

In spite of the deadly work of my grape-gorged carronade, our foe still outnumbered us, I reckoned, by three to one. Honour forbade my fixing it at a lower figure — this was the minimum rate at which one dared to do business with pirates. They were stark veterans, too, every man seamed with ancient sabre-cuts, whereas my crew had many of them hardly attained the maturity which is the gift of ten long summers — and the whole thing was so sudden that I had no time to invent a reinforcement of riper years. It was not surprising, therefore, that my dauntless boarding-party, axe in hand and cutlass between teeth, fought their way to the pirates' deck only to be repulsed again and yet again, and that our planks were soon slippery with our own ungrudged and inexhaustible blood. At this critical point in the conflict, the bo'sun, grasping me by the arm, drew my attention to a magnificent British man-of-war, just hove to in the offing, while the signalman, his glass at his eye, reported that she was inquiring whether we wanted any assistance or preferred to go through with the little job ourselves.

This veiled attempt to share our laurels with us, courteously as it was worded, put me on my mettle. Wiping the blood out of my eyes, I ordered the signalman to reply instantly, with the half-dozen or so of flags that he had at his disposal, that much as we appreciated the valour of the regular service, and the delicacy of spirit that animated its commanders, still this was an orthodox case of the young gentleman-adventurer *versus* the unshaved pirate, and Her Majesty's Marine had nothing to do but to form the usual admiring and applauding background. Then, rallying round me the remnant of my faithful crew, I selected a fresh cutlass (I had worn out three already) and plunged once more into the pleasing carnage.

The result was not long doubtful. Indeed, I could not allow it to be, as I was already getting somewhat bored with the pirate business, and was wanting to get on to something more southern and sensuous. All serious resistance came to an end as soon as I had reached the quarter-deck and cut down the pirate chief — a fine black-bearded fellow in his way, but hardly up to date in his parry-and-thrust business. Those whom our cutlasses had spared were marched out along their own plank, in the approved old fashion; and in time the scuppers relieved the decks of the blood that made traffic temporarily impossible. And all the time the British-man-of-war admired and applauded in the offing.

As soon as we had got through with the necessary throat-cutting and swabbing-up all hands set to work to discover treasure; and soon the deck shone bravely with ingots and Mexican dollars and church plate. There were ropes of pearls, too, and big stacks of *nougat;* and rubies, and gold watches, and Turkish Delight in tubs. But I left these trifles to my crew, and continued the search alone. For by this time I had determined that there should be a Princess on board, carried off to be sold in captivity to the bold bad Moors, and now with beating heart awaiting her rescue by me, the Perseus of her dreams.

I came upon her at last in the big state-cabin in the stern; and she wore a holland pinafore over her Princess-clothes, and she had brown wavy hair, hanging down her back, just like — well, never mind, she had brown wavy hair. When gentle-folk meet, courtesies pass; and I will not weary other people with relating all the compliments and counter-compliments that we exchanged, all in the most approved manner. Occasions like this, when tongues wagged smoothly and speech flowed free, were always especially pleasing to me, who am naturally inclined to be tongue-tied with women. But at last ceremony was over, and we sat on the table and swung our legs and agreed to be fast friends. And I showed her my latest knife — one-bladed, horn-handled, terrific, hung round my neck with string; and she showed me the chiefest treasures the ship contained, hidden away in a most private and particular locker — a musical box with a glass top that let you see the works, and a railway train with real lines and a real tunnel, and a tin iron-clad that followed a magnet, and was ever so much handier in many respects than the real full-sized thing that still lay and applauded in the offing.

There was high feasting that night in my cabin. We invited the captain of the man-of-war — one could hardly do less, it seemed to me — and the Princess took one end of the table and I took the other, and the captain was very kind and nice, and told us fairy-stories, and asked us both to come and stay with him next Christmas, and promised we should have some hunting, on real ponies. When he left I gave him some ingots and things, and saw him into his boat; and then I went round the ship and addressed the crew in several set speeches, which moved them deeply, and with my own hands loaded up the carronade with grape-shot till it ran over at the mouth. This done, I retired into the cabin with the Princess, and

locked the door. And first we started the
musical box, taking turns to wind it up ; and
then we made toffee in the cabin-stove ; and
then we ran the train round and round the room,
and through and through the tunnel ; and lastly
we swam the tin ironclad in the bath, with the
soap-dish for a pirate.

Next morning the air was rich with spices,
porpoises rolled and gambolled round the bows,
and the South Sea Islands lay full in view (they
were the *real* South Sea Islands, of course —
not the badly furnished journeymen-islands that
are to be perceived on the map). As for the
pirate brigantine and the man-of-war, I don't
really know what became of them. They had
played their part very well, for the time, but I
was n't going to bother to account for them, so
I just let them evaporate quietly. The islands
provided plenty of fresh occupation. For here
were little bays of silvery sand, dotted with
land-crabs ; groves of palm-trees wherein mon-
keys frisked and pelted each other with cocoa-
nuts ; and caves, and sites for stockades, and
hidden treasures significantly indicated by skulls,

in riotous plenty; while birds and beasts of every colour and all latitudes made pleasing noises which excited the sporting instinct.

The islands lay conveniently close together, which necessitated careful steering as we threaded the devious and intricate channels that separated them. Of course no one else could be trusted at the wheel, so it is not surprising that for some time I quite forgot that there was such a thing as a Princess on board. This is too much the masculine way, whenever there's any real business doing. However, I remembered her as soon as the anchor was dropped, and I went below and consoled her, and we had breakfast together, and she was allowed to "pour out," which quite made up for everything. When breakfast was over we ordered out the captain's gig, and rowed all about the islands, and paddled, and explored, and hunted bisons and beetles and butterflies, and found everything we wanted. And I gave her pink shells and tortoises and great milky pearls and little green lizards; and she gave me guinea-pigs, and coral to make into waistcoat-buttons, and tame sea-otters, and a real pirate's powder-horn. It was a prolific day and a long-lasting one, and weary were we with all our hunting and our getting and our gathering, when at last we clambered into the captain's gig and rowed back to a late tea.

The following day my conscience rose up and accused me. This was not what I had come out to do. These triflings with pearls and parrakeets, these *al fresco* luncheons off yams and bananas — there was no " making of history " about them. I resolved that without further dallying I would turn to and capture the French frigate, according to the original programme. So we upped anchor with the morning tide, and set all sail for San Salvador.

Of course I had no idea where San Salvador really was. I have n't now, for that matter. But it seemed a right-sounding sort of name for a place that was to have a bay that was to hold a French frigate that was to be cut out ; so, as I said, we sailed for San Salvador, and made the bay about eight bells that evening, and saw the topmasts of the frigate over the headland that sheltered her. And forthwith there was summoned a Council of War.

It is a very serious matter, a Council of War. We had not held one hitherto, pirates and truck of that sort not calling for such solemn treatment. But in an affair that might almost be called international, it seemed well to proceed gravely and by regular steps. So we met in my cabin — the Princess, and the bo'sun, and a boy from the real-life lot, and a man from among the book-men, and a fellow from No-man's-land, and myself in the chair.

The bo'sun had taken part in so many cuttings-out during his past career that practically he did all the talking, and was the Council of War himself. It was to be an affair of boats, he explained. A boat's-crew would be told off to cut the cables, and two boats'-crews to climb stealthily on board and overpower the sleeping Frenchmen, and two more boats'-crews to haul the doomed vessel out of the bay. This made rather a demand on my limited resources as to crews; but I was prepared to stretch a point in a case like this, and I speedily brought my numbers up to the requisite efficiency.

The night was both moonless and starless — I had arranged all that — when the boats pushed off from the side of our vessel, and made their way toward the ship that, unfortunately for itself, had been singled out by Fate to carry me home in triumph. I was in excellent spirits, and, indeed, as I stepped over the side, a lawless idea crossed my mind, of discovering another Princess on board the frigate — a French one this time; I had heard that that sort was rather nice. But I abandoned the notion at once, recollecting that the heroes of all history had always been noted for their unswerving constancy.

The French captain was snug in bed when I clambered in through his cabin window and held a naked cutlass to his throat. Naturally he was surprised and considerably alarmed, till I discharged one of my set speeches at him, pointing out that my men already had his crew under hatchways, that his vessel was even then being towed out of harbour, and that, on his accepting the situation with a good grace, his person and private property would be treated with all the respect due to the representative of a great nation for which I entertained feelings of the profoundest admiration and regard and all that sort of thing. It was a beautiful speech. The Frenchman at once presented me with his parole, in the usual way, and, in a reply of some power and pathos, only begged that I would retire a moment while he put on his trousers. This I gracefully consented to do, and the incident ended.

Two of my boats were sunk by the fire from the forts on the shore, and several brave fellows were severely wounded in the hand-to-hand struggle with the French crew for the possession of the frigate. But the bo'sun's admirable strategy, and my own reckless gallantry in securing the French captain at the outset, had the fortunate result of keeping down the death-rate. It was all for the sake of the Princess that I had arranged so comparatively tame a victory. For myself, I rather liked a fair amount of blood-letting, red-hot shot, and flying splinters. But when you have girls about the place, they have got to be considered to a certain extent.

There was another supper-party that night, in my cabin, as soon as we had got well out to sea; and the French captain, who was the guest of the evening, was in the greatest possible form. We became sworn friends, and exchanged invitations to come and stay at each other's homes, and really it was quite difficult to induce him to take his leave. But at last he and his crew were bundled into their boats; and after I had pressed some pirate bullion upon them — delicately, of course, but in a pleasant manner that admitted of no denial — the gallant fellows quite broke down, and we parted, our bosoms heaving with a full sense of each other's magnanimity and good-fellowship.

The next day, which was nearly all taken up with shifting our quarters into the new frigate, so honourably and easily acquired, was a very pleasant one, as everyone who has gone up in the world and moved into a larger house will readily understand. At last I had grim, black guns all along each side, instead of a rotten

brass carronade; at last I had a square-rigged
ship, with real yards, and a proper quarter-deck.
In fact, now that I had soared as high as could
be hoped in a single voyage, it seemed about
time to go home and cut a dash and show off
a bit. The worst of this ocean-theatre was, it
held no proper audience. It was hard, of course,
to relinquish all the adventures that still lay un-
touched in these Southern seas. Whaling, for
instance, had not yet been entered upon; the
joys of exploration, and strange inland cities
innocent of the white man, still awaited me;
and the book of wrecks and rescues was not yet
even opened. But I had achieved a frigate and
a Princess, and that was not so bad for a beginning, and more than enough to show off with
before those dull unadventurous folk who continued on their mill-horse round at home.

The voyage home was a record one, so far as
mere speed was concerned, and all adventures
were scornfully left behind, as we rattled along,
for other adventurers who had still their laurels
to win. Hardly later than the noon of next day
we dropped anchor in Plymouth Sound, and

heard the intoxicating clamour of bells, the roar of artillery, and the hoarse cheers of an excited populace surging down to the quays, that told us we were being appreciated at something like our true merits. The Lord Mayor was waiting there to receive us, and with him several Admirals of the Fleet, as we walked down the lane of pushing, enthusiastic Devonians, the Princess and I, and our war-worn, weather-beaten, spoil-laden crew. Everybody was very nice about the French frigate, and the pirate booty, and the scars still fresh on our young limbs; yet I think what I liked best of all was, that they all pronounced the Princess to be a duck, and a peerless, brown-haired darling, and a true mate for a hero, and of the right Princess-breed.

The air was thick with invitations and with the smell of civic banquets in a forward stage; but I sternly waved all festivities aside. The coaches-and-four I had ordered immediately on arriving were blocking the whole of the High Street; the champing of bits and the pawing of gravel summoned us to take our seats and be off, to where the real performance awaited us, compared with which all this was but an interlude. I placed the Princess in the most highly gilded coach of the lot, and mounted to my place at her side ; and the rest of the crew scrambled on board of the others as best they might. The whips cracked and the crowd scattered and cheered as we broke into a gallop for home. The noisy bells burst into a farewell peal —

Yes, that was undoubtedly the usual bell for school-room tea. And high time too, I thought, as I tumbled out of the bath, which was beginning to feel very hard to the projecting portions of my frame-work. As I trotted downstairs, hungrier even than usual, farewells floated up from the front door, and I heard the departing voices of our angular elderly visitors as they made their way down the walk. Man was still catching it, apparently — Man was getting it hot. And much Man cared! The seas were his, and their islands ; he had his frigates for the taking, his pirates and their hoards for an unregarded cutlass-stroke or two ; and there were Princesses in plenty waiting for him somewhere — Princesses of the right sort.

THE RELUCTANT DRAGON

"What's your mind always occupied about?" asked the Boy.
"That's what I want to know."

THE RELUCTANT DRAGON

FOOTPRINTS in the snow have been unfailing provokers of sentiment ever since snow was first a white wonder in this drab-coloured world of ours. In a poetry-book presented to one of us by an aunt, there was a poem by one Wordsworth, in which they stood out strongly — with a picture all to themselves, too — but we did n't think very highly either of the poem or the sentiment. Footprints in the sand, now, were quite another matter, and we grasped Crusoe's attitude of mind much more easily than Wordsworth's. Excitement and mystery, curiosity and suspense — these were the only sentiments that tracks, whether in sand or in snow, were able to arouse in us.

We had awakened early that winter morning, puzzled at first by the added light that filled the room. Then, when the truth at last fully dawned on us and we knew that snow-balling was no longer a wistful dream, but a solid certainty waiting for us outside, it was a mere brute fight for the necessary clothes, and the lacing of boots seemed a clumsy invention, and the buttoning of coats an unduly tedious form of fastening, with all that snow going to waste at our very door.

When dinner-time came we had to be dragged in by the scruff of our necks. The short armistice over, the combat was resumed; but presently Charlotte and I, a little weary of contests and of missiles that ran shudderingly down inside one's clothes, forsook the trampled battle-field of the lawn and went exploring the blank virgin spaces of the white world that lay beyond. It stretched away unbroken on every side of us, this mysterious soft garment under which our familiar world had so suddenly hidden itself. Faint imprints showed where a casual bird had alighted, but of other traffic there was next to no sign; which made these strange tracks all the more puzzling.

We came across them first at the corner of the shrubbery, and pored over them long, our

hands on our knees. Experienced trappers that
we knew ourselves to be, it was annoying to be
brought up suddenly by a beast we could not at
once identify.

"Don't you know?" said Charlotte, rather
scornfully. "Thought you knew all the beasts
that ever was."

This put me on my mettle, and I hastily rattled
off a string of animal names embracing both the
arctic and the tropic zones, but without much
real confidence.

"No," said Charlotte, on consideration;
"they won't any of 'em quite do. Seems like
something *lizardy*. Did you say a iguanodon?
Might be that, p'raps. But that's not British,
and we want a real British beast. *I* think it's
a dragon!"

"'T is n't half big enough," I objected.

"Well, all dragons must be small to begin
with," said Charlotte: "like everything else.
P'raps this is a little dragon who's got lost. A
little dragon would be rather nice to have. He
might scratch and spit, but he could n't *do* anything really. Let's track him down!"

So we set off into the wide snow-clad world,
hand in hand, our hearts big with expectation, —
complacently confident that by a few smudgy
traces in the snow we were in a fair way to
capture a half-grown specimen of a fabulous
beast.

We ran the monster across the paddock and
along the hedge of the next field, and then he
took to the road like any tame civilised tax-
payer. Here his tracks became blended with
and lost among more ordinary footprints, but
imagination and a fixed idea will do a great
deal, and we were sure we knew the direction
a dragon would naturally take. The traces,
too, kept reappearing at intervals — at least
Charlotte maintained they did, and as it was
her dragon I left the following of the slot to
her and trotted along peacefully, feeling that
it was an expedition anyhow and something was
sure to come out of it.

Charlotte took me across another field or two,
and through a copse, and into a fresh road ; and
I began to feel sure it was only her confounded
pride that made her go on pretending to see

dragon-tracks instead of owning she was entirely at fault, like a reasonable person. At last she dragged me excitedly through a gap in a hedge of an obviously private character; the waste, open world of field and hedgerow disappeared, and we found ourselves in a garden, well-kept, secluded, most undragon-haunted in appearance. Once inside, I knew where we were. This was the garden of my friend the circus-man, though I had never approached it before by a lawless gap, from this unfamiliar side. And here was the circus-man himself, placidly smoking a pipe as he strolled up and down the walks. I stepped up to him and asked him politely if he had lately seen a Beast.

"May I inquire," he said, with all civility, "what particular sort of a Beast you may happen to be looking for?"

"It's a *lizardy* sort of Beast," I explained. "Charlotte says it's a dragon, but she doesn't really know much about beasts."

The circus-man looked round about him slowly. "I don't *think*," he said, "that I've seen a dragon in these parts recently. But if I come

across one I 'll know it belongs to you, and I 'll
have him taken round to you at once."

" Thank you very much," said Charlotte,
" but don't *trouble* about it, please, 'cos p'raps
it is n't a dragon, after all. Only I thought I
saw his little footprints in the snow, and we
followed 'em up, and they seemed to lead right
in here, but maybe it 's all a mistake, and thank
you all the same."

" Oh, no trouble at all," said the circus-man,
cheerfully. " I should be only too pleased.
But of course, as you say, it *may* be a mistake.
And it 's getting dark, and he seems to have got
away for the present, whatever he is. You 'd
better come in and have some tea. I 'm quite
alone, and we 'll make a roaring fire, and I 've
got the biggest Book of Beasts you ever saw.
It 's got every beast in the world, and all of 'em
coloured ; and we 'll try and find *your* beast
in it ! "

We were always ready for tea at any time,
and especially when combined with beasts.
There was marmalade, too, and apricot-jam,
brought in expressly for us ; and afterwards

the beast-book was spread out, and, as the man had truly said, it contained every sort of beast that had ever been in the world.

The striking of six o'clock set the more prudent Charlotte nudging me, and we recalled ourselves with an effort from Beastland, and reluctantly stood up to go.

"Here, I'm coming along with you," said the circus-man. "I want another pipe, and a walk'll do me good. You needn't talk to me unless you like."

Our spirits rose to their wonted level again. The way had seemed so long, the outside world so dark and eerie, after the bright warm room and the highly-coloured beast-book. But a walk with a real Man — why, that was a treat in itself! We set off briskly, the Man in the middle. I looked up at him and wondered whether I should ever live to smoke a big pipe with that careless sort of majesty! But Charlotte, whose young mind was not set on tobacco as a possible goal, made herself heard from the other side.

"Now, then," she said, "tell us a story, please, won't you?"

The Man sighed heavily and looked about him. "I knew it," he groaned. "I *knew* I should have to tell a story. Oh, why did I leave my pleasant fireside? Well, I *will* tell you a story. Only let me think a minute."

So he thought a minute, and then he told us this story.

Long ago — might have been hundreds of years ago — in a cottage half-way between this village and yonder shoulder of the Downs up there, a shepherd lived with his wife and their little son. Now the shepherd spent his days — and at certain times of the year his nights too — up on the wide ocean-bosom of the Downs, with only the sun and the stars and the sheep for company, and the friendly chattering world of men and women far out of sight and hearing. But his little son, when he wasn't helping his father, and often when he was as well, spent much of his time buried in big volumes that he borrowed from the affable gentry and interested parsons of the country round about. And his parents were very fond of him, and rather proud of him too, though they did n't let on in his hearing, so he was left to go his own way and read as much as he liked ; and instead of frequently getting a cuff on the side of the head, as might very well have happened to him, he was treated more or less as an equal by his parents, who sensibly thought it a very fair division of labour that they should supply the practical knowledge, and he the book-learning. They knew that book-learning often came in useful at a pinch, in spite of what their neighbours said. What the Boy chiefly dabbled in was natural history and fairy-tales, and he just took them as they came, in a sandwichy sort of way, without making any distinctions ; and really his course of reading strikes one as rather sensible.

One evening the shepherd, who for some nights past had been disturbed and preoccupied, and off his usual mental balance, came home all of a tremble, and, sitting down at the table where his wife and son were peacefully employed, she with her seam, he in following out the adventures of the Giant with no Heart in his Body, exclaimed with much agitation :

"It's all up with me, Maria! Never no more can I go up on them there Downs, was it ever so!"

"Now don't you take on like that," said his wife, who was a *very* sensible woman: "but tell us all about it first, whatever it is as has given you this shake-up, and then me and you and the son here, between us, we ought to be able to get to the bottom of it!"

"It began some nights ago," said the shepherd. "You know that cave up there — I never liked it, somehow, and the sheep never liked it neither, and when sheep don't like a thing there's generally some reason for it. Well, for some time past there's been faint noises coming from that cave — noises like heavy sighings, with grunts mixed up in them; and sometimes a snoring, far away down — *real* snoring, yet somehow not *honest* snoring, like you and me o' nights, you know!"

"*I* know," remarked the Boy, quietly.

"Of course I was terrible frightened," the shepherd went on; "yet somehow I couldn't keep away. So this very evening, before I come down, I took a cast round by the cave, quietly. And there — O Lord! there I saw him at last, as plain as I see you!"

"Saw *who?*" said his wife, beginning to share in her husband's nervous terror.

"Why *him*, I'm a telling you!" said the shepherd. "He was sticking half-way out of the cave, and seemed to be enjoying of the cool of the evening in a poetical sort of way. He was as big as four cart-horses, and all covered with shiny scales — deep-blue scales at the top of him, shading off to a tender sort o' green below. As he breathed, there was that sort of flicker over his nostrils that you see over our chalk roads on a baking windless day in summer. He had his chin on his paws, and I should say he was meditating about things. Oh, yes, a peaceable sort o' beast enough, and not ramping or carrying on or doing anything but what was quite right and proper. I admit all that. And yet, what am I to do? *Scales*, you know, and claws, and a tail for certain, though I didn't see that end of him — I ain't *used* to 'em, and I don't *hold* with 'em, and that's a fact!"

The Boy, who had apparently been absorbed in his book during his father's recital, now closed the volume, yawned, clasped his hands behind his head, and said sleepily:

"It's all right, father. Don't you worry. It's only a dragon."

"Only a dragon?" cried his father. "What do you mean, sitting there, you and your dragons? *Only* a dragon indeed! And what do *you* know about it?"

"'Cos it *is*, and 'cos I *do* know," replied the Boy, quietly. "Look here, father, you know we've each of us got our line. *You* know about sheep, and weather, and things; *I* know about dragons. I always said, you know, that that cave up there was a dragon-cave. I always said it must have belonged to a dragon some time, and ought to belong to a dragon now, if rules count for anything. Well, now you tell me it *has* got a dragon, and so *that's* all right. I'm not half as much surprised as when you told me it *had n't* got a dragon. Rules always come right if you wait quietly. Now, please, just leave this all to me. And I'll stroll up to-morrow morning — no, in the morning I can't, I've got a whole heap of things to do — well, perhaps in the evening, if I'm quite free, I'll go up and have a talk to him, and you'll find it'll be all right. Only, please, don't you go worrying round there without me. You don't understand 'em a bit, and they're very sensitive, you know!''

"He's quite right, father," said the sensible mother. "As he says, dragons is his line and not ours. He's wonderful knowing about book-beasts, as every one allows. And to tell the truth, I'm not half happy in my own mind, thinking of that poor animal lying alone up there, without a bit o' hot supper or anyone to change the news with; and maybe we'll be able to do something for him; and if he ain't quite respectable our Boy'll find it out quick enough. He's got a pleasant sort o' way with him that makes everybody tell him everything.''

Next day, after he'd had his tea, the Boy strolled up the chalky track that led to the summit of the Downs; and there, sure enough, he found the dragon, stretched lazily on the sward in front of his cave. The view from that point was a magnificent one. To the right and left, the bare and willowy leagues of Downs; in front, the vale, with its clustered homesteads, its threads of white roads running through orchards and well-tilled acreage, and, far away, a hint of grey old cities on the horizon. A cool breeze played over the surface of the grass and the silver shoulder of a large moon was showing above distant junipers. No wonder the dragon seemed in a peaceful and contented mood; indeed, as the Boy approached he could hear the beast purring with a happy regularity. " Well, we live and learn!" he said to himself. " None of my books ever told me that dragons purred!"

" Hullo, dragon!" said the Boy, quietly, when he had got up to him.

The dragon, on hearing the approaching footsteps, made the beginning of a courteous effort to rise. But when he saw it was a Boy, he set his eyebrows severely.

" Now don't you hit me," he said; "or bung stones, or squirt water, or anything. I won't have it, I tell you!"

"Not goin' to hit you," said the Boy, wearily, dropping on the grass beside the beast: "and don't, for goodness' sake, keep on saying 'Don't;' I hear so much of it, and it's monotonous, and makes me tired. I've simply looked in to ask you how you were and all that sort of thing; but if I'm in the way I can easily clear out. I've lots of friends, and no one can say I'm in the habit of shoving myself in where I'm not wanted!"

"No, no, don't go off in a huff," said the dragon, hastily; "fact is, — I'm as happy up here as the day's long; never without an occupation, dear fellow, never without an occupation! And yet, between ourselves, it *is* a trifle dull at times."

The Boy bit off a stalk of grass and chewed it. "Going to make a long stay here?" he asked, politely.

"Can't hardly say at present," replied the dragon. "It seems a nice place enough — but I've only been here a short time, and one must look about and reflect and consider before settling down. It's rather a serious thing, settling down. Besides — now I'm going to tell you something! You'd never guess it if you tried ever so! — fact is, I'm such a confoundedly lazy beggar!'"

"You surprise me," said the Boy, civilly.

"It's the sad truth," the dragon went on, settling down between his paws and evidently delighted to have found a listener at last: "and I fancy that's really how I came to be here. You see all the other fellows were so active and *earnest* and all that sort of thing — always rampaging, and skirmishing, and scouring the desert sands, and pacing the margin of the sea, and chasing knights all over the place, and devouring damsels, and going on generally — whereas I liked to get my meals regular and then to prop my back against a bit of rock and snooze a bit, and wake up and think of things going on and how they kept going on just the same, you know! So when it happened I got fairly caught."

"When *what* happened, please?" asked the Boy.

"That's just what I don't precisely know,"

said the dragon. " I suppose the earth sneezed, or shook itself, or the bottom dropped out of something. Anyhow there was a shake and a roar and a general stramash, and I found myself miles away underground and wedged in as tight as tight. Well, thank goodness, my wants are few, and at any rate I had peace and quietness and was n't always being asked to come along and *do* something. And I 've got such an active mind—always occupied, I assure you! But time went on, and there was a certain sameness about the life, and at last I began to think it would be fun to work my way upstairs and see what you other fellows were doing. So I scratched and burrowed, and worked this way and that way and at last I came out through this cave here. And I like the country, and the view, and the people — what I 've seen of 'em — and on the whole I feel inclined to settle down here."

" What 's your mind always occupied about?" asked the Boy. " That 's what I want to know."

The dragon coloured slightly and looked away. Presently he said bashfully :

"Did you ever — just for fun — try to make up poetry — verses, you know?"

"'Course I have," said the Boy. "Heaps of it. And some of it's quite good, I feel sure, only there's no one here cares about it. Mother's very kind and all that, when I read it to her, and so's father for that matter. But somehow they don't seem to — "

"Exactly," cried the dragon; "my own case exactly. They don't seem to, and you can't argue with 'em about it. Now you've got culture, you have, I could tell it on you at once, and I should just like your candid opinion about some little things I threw off lightly, when I was down there. I'm awfully pleased to have met you, and I'm hoping the other neighbours will be equally agreeable. There was a very nice old gentleman up here only last night, but he didn't seem to want to intrude."

"That was my father," said the Boy, "and he *is* a nice old gentleman, and I'll introduce you some day if you like."

"Can't you two come up here and dine or something to-morrow?" asked the dragon, eagerly. " Only, of course, if you 've got nothing better to do," he added politely.

" Thanks awfully," said the Boy, " but we don't go out anywhere without my mother, and, to tell you the truth, I 'm afraid she might n't quite approve of you. You see there 's no getting over the hard fact that you 're a dragon, is there? And when you talk of settling down, and the neighbours, and so on, I can't help feeling that you don't quite realise your position. You 're an enemy of the human race, you see ! "

" Have n't got an enemy in the world," said the dragon, cheerfully. " Too lazy to make 'em, to begin with. And if I *do* read other fellows my poetry, I 'm always ready to listen to theirs ! "

" Oh, dear ! " cried the Boy, " I wish you 'd try and grasp the situation properly. When the other people find you out, they 'll come after you with spears and swords and all sorts of things. You 'll have to be exterminated, according to their way of looking at it ! You 're a scourge, and a pest, and a baneful monster ! "

" Not a word of truth in it," said the dragon,

wagging his head solemnly. " Character 'll bear the strictest investigation. And now, there 's a little sonnet-thing I was working on when you appeared on the scene — "

" Oh, if you *won't* be sensible," cried the Boy, getting up, " I 'm going off home. No, I can't stop for sonnets ; my mother 's sitting up. I 'll look you up to-morrow, sometime or other, and do for goodness' sake try and realise that you 're a pestilential scourge, or you 'll find yourself in a most awful fix. Good-night ! "

The Boy found it an easy matter to set the mind of his parents at ease about his new friend. They had always left that branch to him, and they took his word without a murmur. The shepherd was formally introduced and many compliments and kind inquiries were exchanged. His wife, however, though expressing her willingness to do anything she could, — to mend things, or set the cave to rights, or cook a little something when the dragon had been poring over sonnets and forgotten his meals, as male things *will* do, — could not be brought to recognise him formally. The fact that he was a dragon and "they did n't know who he was" seemed to count for everything with her. She made no objection, however, to her little son spending his evenings with the dragon quietly, so long as he was home by nine o'clock : and many a pleasant night they had, sitting on the sward, while the dragon told stories of old, old times, when dragons were quite plentiful and the world was a livelier place than it is now, and life was full of thrills and jumps and surprises.

What the Boy had feared, however, soon came to pass. The most modest and retiring dragon in the world, if he's as big as four cart-horses and covered with blue scales, cannot keep altogether out of the public view. And so in the village tavern of nights the fact that a real live dragon sat brooding in the cave on the Downs was naturally a subject for talk. Though the villagers were extremely frightened, they were rather proud as well. It was a dis-tinction to have a dragon of your own, and it was felt to be a feather in the cap of the village. Still, all were agreed that this sort of thing could n't be allowed to go on. The dreadful beast must be exterminated, the country-side must be freed from this pest, this terror, this destroying scourge. The fact that not even a hen-roost was the worse for the dragon's arrival wasn't allowed to have anything to do with it. He was a dragon, and he couldn't deny it, and if he didn't choose to behave as such that was his own lookout. But in spite of much valiant talk no hero was found willing to take sword and spear and free the suffering village and win deathless fame; and each night's heated discussion always ended in nothing. Meanwhile the dragon, a happy Bohemian, lolled on the turf, enjoyed the sunsets, told antediluvian anecdotes to the Boy, and polished his old verses while meditating on fresh ones.

One day the Boy, on walking in to the village, found everything wearing a festal appearance which was not to be accounted for in the calendar. Carpets and gay-coloured stuffs were hung out of the windows, the church-bells clamoured noisily, the little street was flower-strewn, and the whole population jostled each other along either side of it, chattering, shoving, and ordering each other to stand back. The Boy saw a friend of his own age in the crowd and hailed him.

"What's up?" he cried. "Is it the players, or bears, or a circus, or what?"

"It's all right," his friend hailed back. "He's a-coming."

"*Who's* a-coming?" demanded the Boy, thrusting into the throng.

"Why, St. George, of course," replied his friend. "He's heard tell of our dragon, and he's comin' on purpose to slay the deadly beast, and free us from his horrid yoke. O my! won't there be a jolly fight!"

Here was news indeed! The Boy felt that he ought to make quite sure for himself, and he wriggled himself in between the legs of his good-natured elders, abusing them all the time for their unmannerly habit of shoving. Once in the front rank, he breathlessly awaited the arrival.

Presently from the far-away end of the line came the sound of cheering. Next, the measured tramp of a great war-horse made his heart beat quicker, and then he found himself cheering with the rest, as, amidst welcoming shouts, shrill cries of women, uplifting of babies and waving of handkerchiefs, St. George paced slowly up the street. The Boy's heart stood still and he breathed with sobs, the beauty and the grace of the hero were so far beyond anything he had yet seen. His fluted armour was inlaid with gold, his plumed helmet hung at his saddle-bow, and his thick fair hair framed a face gracious and gentle beyond expression till you caught the sternness in his eyes. He drew rein in front of the little inn, and the villagers crowded round with greetings and thanks and voluble statements of their wrongs and grievances and oppressions. The Boy heard the grave gentle voice of the Saint, assuring them that all would be well now, and that he would stand by them and see them righted and free them from their foe; then he dismounted and passed through the doorway and the crowd poured in after him. But the Boy made off up the hill as fast as he could lay his legs to the ground.

"It's all up, dragon!" he shouted as soon as he was within sight of the beast. "He's coming! He's here now! You'll have to pull yourself together and *do* something at last!"

The dragon was licking his scales and rubbing them with a bit of house-flannel the Boy's mother had lent him, till he shone like a great turquoise.

" Don't be *violent*, Boy," he said without looking round. " Sit down and get your breath, and try and remember that the noun governs the verb, and then perhaps you'll be good enough to tell me *who's* coming?"

" That's right, take it coolly," said the Boy. " Hope you'll be half as cool when I've got through with my news. It's only St. George who's coming, that's all; he rode into the village half-an-hour ago. Of course you can lick him — a great big fellow like you! But I thought I'd warn you, 'cos he's sure to be round early, and he's got the longest, wickedest-looking spear you ever did see!" And the Boy got up and began to jump round in sheer delight at the prospect of the battle.

" O deary, deary me," moaned the dragon; " this is too awful. I won't see him, and that's flat. I don't want to know the fellow at all.

I'm sure he's not nice. You must tell him to go away at once, please. Say he can write if he likes, but I can't give him an interview. I'm not seeing anybody at present."

"Now dragon, dragon," said the Boy, imploringly, "don't be perverse and wrongheaded. You've *got* to fight him some time or other, you know, 'cos he's St. George and you're the dragon. Better get it over, and then we can go on with the sonnets. And you ought to consider other people a little, too. If it's been dull up here for you, think how dull it's been for me!"

"My dear little man," said the dragon, solemnly, "just understand, once for all, that I can't fight and I won't fight. I've never fought in my life, and I'm not going to begin now, just to give you a Roman holiday. In old days I always let the other fellows — the *earnest* fellows — do all the fighting, and no doubt that's why I have the pleasure of being here now."

"But if you don't fight he'll cut your head off!" gasped the Boy, miserable at the prospect of losing both his fight and his friend.

"Oh, I think not," said the dragon in his lazy way. "You'll be able to arrange something. I've every confidence in you, you're such a *manager*. Just run down, there's a dear chap, and make it all right. I leave it entirely to you."

The Boy made his way back to the village in a state of great despondency. First of all, there wasn't going to be any fight ; next, his dear and honoured friend the dragon hadn't shown up in quite such a heroic light as he would have liked ; and lastly, whether the dragon was a hero at heart or not, it made no difference, for St. George would most undoubtedly cut his head off. "Arrange things indeed!" he said bitterly to himself. "The dragon treats the whole affair as if it was an invitation to tea and croquet."

The villagers were straggling homewards as he passed up the street, all of them in the highest spirits, and gleefully discussing the splendid fight that was in store. The Boy pursued his way to the inn, and passed into the principal chamber, where St. George now sat alone, musing over the chances of the fight, and the

sad stories of rapine and of wrong that had so
lately been poured into his sympathetic ears.

"May I come in, St. George?" said the Boy,
politely, as he paused at the door. "I want to
talk to you about this little matter of the dragon,
if you're not tired of it by this time."

"Yes, come in, Boy," said the Saint, kindly.
"Another tale of misery and wrong, I fear me.
Is it a kind parent, then, of whom the tyrant has
bereft you? Or some tender sister or brother?
Well, it shall soon be avenged."

"Nothing of the sort," said the Boy. "There's
a misunderstanding somewhere, and I want to
put it right. The fact is, this is a *good* dragon."

"Exactly," said St. George, smiling pleasantly, "I quite understand. A good *dragon.*
Believe me, I do not in the least regret that he
is an adversary worthy of my steel, and no feeble
specimen of his noxious tribe."

"But he's *not* a noxious tribe," cried the
Boy, distressedly. "Oh dear, oh dear, how
stupid men are when they get an idea into their
heads! I tell you he's a *good* dragon, and a
friend of mine, and tells me the most beautiful

stories you ever heard, all about old times and
when he was little. And he's been so kind to
mother, and mother'd do anything for him. And
father likes him too, though father does n't hold
with art and poetry much, and always falls
asleep when the dragon starts talking about
style. But the fact is, nobody can help liking
him when once they know him. He's so en-
gaging and so trustful, and as simple as a child!"

" Sit down, and draw your chair up," said
St. George. " I like a fellow who sticks up for
his friends, and I'm sure the dragon has his
good points, if he's got a friend like you. But
that's not the question. All this evening I've
been listening, with grief and anguish unspeak-
able, to tales of murder, theft, and wrong ; rather
too highly coloured, perhaps, not always quite
convincing, but forming in the main a most
serious roll of crime. History teaches us that
the greatest rascals often possess all the domestic
virtues ; and I fear that your cultivated friend,
in spite of the qualities which have won (and
rightly) your regard, has got to be speedily
exterminated."

"Oh, you've been taking in all the yarns those fellows have been telling you," said the Boy, impatiently. "Why, our villagers are the biggest story-tellers in all the country round. It's a known fact. You're a stranger in these parts, or else you'd have heard it already. All they want is a *fight*. They're the most awful beggars for getting up fights — it's meat and drink to them. Dogs, bulls, dragons — anything so long as it's a fight. Why, they've got a poor innocent badger in the stable behind here, at this moment. They were going to have some fun with him to-day, but they're saving him up now till *your* little affair's over. And I've no doubt they've been telling you what a hero you were, and how you were bound to win, in the cause of right and justice, and so on; but let me tell you, I came down the street just now, and they were betting six to four on the dragon freely!"

"Six to four on the dragon!" murmured St. George, sadly, resting his cheek on his hand. "This is an evil world, and sometimes I begin to think that all the wickedness in it is not entirely bottled up inside the dragons. And yet —may not this wily beast have misled you as to his real character, in order that your good report of him may serve as a cloak for his evil deeds? Nay, may there not be, at this very moment, some hapless Princess immured within yonder gloomy cavern?"

The moment he had spoken, St. George was sorry for what he had said, the Boy looked so genuinely distressed.

"I assure you, St. George," he said earnestly, "there's nothing of the sort in the cave at all. The dragon's a real gentleman, every inch of him, and I may say that no one would be more shocked and grieved than he would, at hearing you talk in that—that *loose* way about matters on which he has very strong views!"

"Well, perhaps I've been over-credulous," said St. George. "Perhaps I've misjudged the animal. But what are we to do? Here are the dragon and I, almost face to face, each supposed to be thirsting for each other's blood. I don't see any way out of it, exactly. What do you suggest? Can't you arrange things, somehow?"

"That's just what the dragon said," replied the Boy, rather nettled. "Really, the way you two seem to leave everything to me — I suppose you couldn't be persuaded to go away quietly, could you?"

"Impossible, I fear," said the Saint. "Quite against the rules. *You* know that as well as I do."

"Well, then, look here," said the Boy, "it's early yet — would you mind strolling up with me and seeing the dragon and talking it over? It's not far, and any friend of mine will be most welcome."

"Well, it's *irregular*," said St. George, rising, "but really it seems about the most sensible thing to do. You're taking a lot of trouble on your friend's account," he added, good-naturedly, as they passed out through the door together. "But cheer up! Perhaps there won't have to be any fight after all."

"Oh, but I hope there will, though!" replied the little fellow, wistfully.

"I've brought a friend to see you, dragon," said the Boy, rather loud.

The dragon woke up with a start. "I was just — er — thinking about things," he said in his simple way. "Very pleased to make your acquaintance, sir. Charming weather we're having!"

"This is St. George," said the Boy, shortly. "St. George, let me introduce you to the dragon. We've come up to talk things over quietly, dragon, and now for goodness' sake do let us have a little straight common-sense, and come to some practical business-like arrangement, for I'm sick of views and theories of life and personal tendencies, and all that sort of thing. I may perhaps add that my mother's sitting up."

"So glad to meet you, St. George," began the dragon, rather nervously, "because you've been a great traveller, I hear, and I've always been rather a stay-at-home. But I can show you many antiquities, many interesting features of our country-side, if you're stopping here any time —"

"I think," said St. George, in his frank,

pleasant way, "that we'd really better take the advice of our young friend here, and try to come to some understanding, on a business footing, about this little affair of ours. Now don't you think that after all the simplest plan would be just to fight it out, according to the rules, and let the best man win? They're betting on you, I may tell you, down in the village, but I don't mind that!"

"Oh, yes, *do*, dragon," said the Boy, delightedly; "it'll save such a lot of bother!"

"My young friend, you shut up," said the dragon, severely. "Believe me, St. George," he went on, "there's nobody in the world I'd sooner oblige than you and this young gentleman here. But the whole thing's nonsense, and conventionality, and popular thick-headedness. There's absolutely nothing to fight about, from beginning to end. And anyhow I'm not going to, so that settles it!"

"But supposing I make you?" said St. George, rather nettled.

"You can't," said the dragon, triumphantly. "I should only go into my cave and retire for a time down the hole I came up. You'd soon get heartily sick of sitting outside and waiting for me to come out and fight you. And as soon as you'd really gone away, why, I'd come up again gaily, for I tell you frankly, I like this place, and I'm going to stay here!"

St. George gazed for a while on the fair landscape around them. "But this would be a beautiful place for a fight," he began again persuasively. "These great bare rolling Downs for the arena, — and me in my golden armour showing up against your big blue scaly coils! Think what a picture it would make!"

"Now you're trying to get at me through my artistic sensibilities," said the dragon. "But it won't work. Not but what it would make a very pretty picture, as you say," he added, wavering a little.

"We seem to be getting rather nearer to *business*," put in the Boy. "You must see, dragon, that there's got to be a fight of some sort, 'cos you can't want to have to go down that dirty old hole again and stop there till goodness knows when."

"It might be arranged," said St. George, thoughtfully. "I *must* spear you somewhere, of course, but I'm not bound to hurt you very much. There's such a lot of you that there must be a few *spare* places somewhere. Here, for instance, just behind your foreleg. It couldn't hurt you much, just here!"

"Now you're tickling, George," said the dragon, coyly. "No, that place won't do at all. Even if it didn't hurt,—and I'm sure it would, awfully,—it would make me laugh, and that would spoil everything."

"Let's try somewhere else, then," said St. George, patiently. "Under your neck, for instance,—all these folds of thick skin,—if I speared you here you'd never even know I'd done it!"

"Yes, but are you sure you can hit off the right place?" asked the dragon, anxiously.

"Of course I am," said St. George, with confidence. "You leave that to me!"

"It's just because I've *got* to leave it to you that I'm asking," replied the dragon, rather testily. "No doubt you would deeply regret any error you might make in the hurry of the moment ; but you would n't regret it half as much as I should ! However, I suppose we 've got to trust somebody, as we go through life, and your plan seems, on the whole, as good a one as any."

"Look here, dragon," interrupted the Boy, a little jealous on behalf of his friend, who seemed to be getting all the worst of the bargain : "I don't quite see where *you* come in ! There 's to be a fight, apparently, and you 're to be licked ; and what I want to know is, what are *you* going to get out of it ?"

"St. George," said the dragon, "just tell him, please, — what will happen after I 'm vanquished in the deadly combat ?"

"Well, according to the rules I suppose I shall lead you in triumph down to the market-place or whatever answers to it," said St. George.

"Precisely," said the dragon. "And then —"

"And then there 'll be shoutings and speeches and things," continued St. George. "And I shall explain that you 're converted, and see the error of your ways, and so on."

" Quite so," said the dragon. " And then — ? "

" Oh, and then — " said St. George, " why, and then there will be the usual banquet, I suppose."

" Exactly," said the dragon; " and that's where *I* come in. Look here," he continued, addressing the Boy, " I'm bored to death up here, and no one really appreciates me. I'm going into Society, I am, through the kindly aid of our friend here, who's taking such a lot of trouble on my account; and you'll find I've got all the qualities to endear me to people who entertain! So now that's all settled, and if you don't mind — I'm an old-fashioned fellow — don't want to turn you out, but — "

" Remember, you'll have to do your proper share of the fighting, dragon! " said St. George, as he took the hint and rose to go; " I mean ramping, and breathing fire, and so on! "

" I can *ramp* all right," replied the dragon, confidently; " as to breathing fire, it's surprising how easily one gets out of practice; but I'll do the best I can. Good-night! "

They had descended the hill and were almost

back in the village again, when St. George stopped short, "*Knew* I had forgotten something," he said. "There ought to be a Princess. Terror-stricken and chained to a rock, and all that sort of thing. Boy, can't you arrange a Princess?"

The Boy was in the middle of a tremendous yawn. "I'm tired to death," he wailed, "and I *can't* arrange a Princess, or anything more, at this time of night. And my mother's sitting up, and *do* stop asking me to arrange more things till to-morrow!"

Next morning the people began streaming up to the Downs at quite an early hour, in their Sunday clothes and carrying baskets with bottle-necks sticking out of them, every one intent on securing good places for the combat. This was not exactly a simple matter, for of course it was quite possible that the dragon might win, and in that case even those who had put their money on him felt they could hardly expect him to deal with his backers on a different footing to the rest. Places were chosen, therefore, with cir-

cumspection and with a view to a speedy retreat
in case of emergency; and the front rank was
mostly composed of boys who had escaped from
parental control and now sprawled and rolled
about on the grass, regardless of the shrill
threats and warnings discharged at them by
their anxious mothers behind.

The Boy had secured a good front place, well
up towards the cave, and was feeling as anxious
as a stage-manager on a first night. Could the
dragon be depended upon? He might change
his mind and vote the whole performance rot;
or else, seeing that the affair had been so hastily
planned, without even a rehearsal, he might be
too nervous to show up. The Boy looked nar-
rowly at the cave, but it showed no sign of life
or occupation. Could the dragon have made a
moon-light flitting?

The higher portions of the ground were now
black with sightseers, and presently a sound of
cheering and a waving of handkerchiefs told that
something was visible to them which the Boy,
far up towards the dragon-end of the line as he
was, could not yet see. A minute more and

THE RELUCTANT DRAGON

St. George's red plumes topped the hill, as the Saint rode slowly forth on the great level space which stretched up to the grim mouth of the cave. Very gallant and beautiful he looked, on his tall war-horse, his golden armour glancing in the sun, his great spear held erect, the little white pennon, crimson-crossed, fluttering at its point. He drew rein and remained motionless. The lines of spectators began to give back a little, nervously ; and even the boys in front stopped pulling hair and cuffing each other, and leaned forward expectant.

" Now then, dragon ! " muttered the Boy, impatiently, fidgeting where he sat. He need not have distressed himself, had he only known. The dramatic possibilities of the thing had tickled the dragon immensely, and he had been up from an early hour, preparing for his first public appearance with as much heartiness as if the years had run backwards, and he had been again a little dragonlet, playing with his sisters on the floor of their mother's cave, at the game of saints-and-dragons, in which the dragon was bound to win.

A low muttering, mingled with snorts, now made itself heard; rising to a bellowing roar that seemed to fill the plain. Then a cloud of smoke obscured the mouth of the cave, and out of the midst of it the dragon himself, shining, sea-blue, magnificent, pranced splendidly forth; and everybody said, " Oo-oo-oo!" as if he had been a mighty rocket! His scales were glittering, his long spiky tail lashed his sides, his claws tore up the turf and sent it flying high over his back, and smoke and fire incessantly jetted from his angry nostrils. " Oh, well done, dragon!" cried the Boy, excitedly. " Did n't think he had it in him!" he added to himself.

St. George lowered his spear, bent his head, dug his heels into his horse's sides, and came thundering over the turf. The dragon charged with a roar and a squeal, — a great blue whirling combination of coils and snorts and clashing jaws and spikes and fire.

" Missed!" yelled the crowd. There was a moment's entanglement of golden armour and blue-green coils, and spiky tail, and then the great horse, tearing at his bit, carried the Saint, his spear swung high in the air, almost up to the mouth of the cave.

The dragon sat down and barked viciously, while St. George with difficulty pulled his horse round into position.

" End of Round One!" thought the Boy. " How well they managed it! But I hope the Saint won't get excited. I can trust the dragon all right. What a regular play-actor the fellow is!"

St. George had at last prevailed on his horse to stand steady, and was looking round him as he wiped his brow. Catching sight of the Boy, he smiled and nodded, and held up three fingers for an instant.

" It seems to be all planned out," said the Boy to himself. " Round Three is to be the finishing one, evidently. Wish it could have lasted a bit longer. Whatever's that old fool of a dragon up to now?"

The dragon was employing the interval in giving a ramping-performance for the benefit of the crowd. Ramping, it should be explained, consists in running round and round in a wide

circle, and sending waves and ripples of movement along the whole length of your spine, from
your pointed ears right down to the spike at the
end of your long tail. When you are covered
with blue scales, the effect is particularly pleasing; and the Boy recollected the dragon's
recently expressed wish to become a social
success.

St. George now gathered up his reins and
began to move forward, dropping the point of
his spear and settling himself firmly in the
saddle.

"Time!" yelled everybody excitedly; and
the dragon, leaving off his ramping, sat up on
end, and began to leap from one side to the
other with huge ungainly bounds, whooping like
a Red Indian. This naturally disconcerted the
horse, who swerved violently, the Saint only just
saving himself by the mane; and as they shot
past the dragon delivered a vicious snap at the
horse's tail which sent the poor beast careering
madly far over the Downs, so that the language
of the Saint, who had lost a stirrup, was fortunately inaudible to the general assemblage.

Round Two evoked audible evidence of friendly feeling towards the dragon. The spectators were not slow to appreciate a combatant who could hold his own so well and clearly wanted to show good sport; and many encouraging remarks reached the ears of our friend as he strutted to and fro, his chest thrust out and his tail in the air, hugely enjoying his new popularity.

St. George had dismounted and was tightening his girths, and telling his horse, with quite an Oriental flow of imagery, exactly what he thought of him, and his relations, and his conduct on the present occasion; so the Boy made his way down to the Saint's end of the line, and held his spear for him.

"It's been a jolly fight, St. George!" he said with a sigh. "Can't you let it last a bit longer?"

"Well, I think I'd better not," replied the Saint. "The fact is, your simple-minded old friend's getting conceited, now they've begun cheering him, and he'll forget all about the arrangement and take to playing the fool, and there's no telling where he would stop. I'll just finish him off this round."

He swung himself into the saddle and took his spear from the Boy. "Now don't you be afraid," he added kindly. "I've marked my spot exactly, and *he's* sure to give me all the assistance in his power, because he knows it's his only chance of being asked to the banquet!"

St. George now shortened his spear, bringing the butt well up under his arm; and, instead of galloping as before, trotted smartly towards the dragon, who crouched at his approach, flicking his tail till it cracked in the air like a great cart-whip. The Saint wheeled as he neared his opponent and circled warily round him, keeping his eye on the spare place; while the dragon, adopting similar tactics, paced with caution round the same circle, occasionally feinting with his head. So the two sparred for an opening, while the spectators maintained a breathless silence.

Though the round lasted for some minutes, the end was so swift that all the Boy saw was a lightning movement of the Saint's arm, and then a whirl and a confusion of spines, claws, tail, and flying bits of turf. The dust cleared away, the spectators whooped and ran in cheering, and the Boy made out that the dragon was down, pinned to the earth by the spear, while St. George had dismounted, and stood astride of him.

It all seemed so genuine that the Boy ran in breathlessly, hoping the dear old dragon wasn't really hurt. As he approached, the dragon lifted one large eyelid, winked solemnly, and collapsed again. He was held fast to earth by the neck, but the Saint had hit him in the spare place agreed upon, and it didn't even seem to tickle.

" Bain't you goin' to cut 'is 'ed orf, master?" asked one of the applauding crowd. He had backed the dragon, and naturally felt a trifle sore.

" Well, not *to-day*, I think," replied St. George, pleasantly. " You see, that can be done at *any* time. There's no hurry at all. I think we'll all go down to the village first, and have some refreshment, and then I'll give him a good talking-to, and you'll find he'll be a very different dragon!"

At that magic word *refreshment* the whole crowd formed up in procession and silently awaited the signal to start. The time for talking and cheering and betting was past, the hour for action had arrived. St. George, hauling on his spear with both hands, released the dragon, who rose and shook himself and ran his eye over his spikes and scales and things, to see that they were all in order. Then the Saint mounted and led off the procession, the dragon following meekly in the company of the Boy, while the thirsty spectators kept at a respectful interval behind.

There were great doings when they got down to the village again, and had formed up in front of the inn. After refreshment St. George made a speech, in which he informed his audience that he had removed their direful scourge, at a great deal of trouble and inconvenience to himself, and now they weren't to go about grumbling and fancying they'd got grievances, because they hadn't. And they shouldn't be so fond of fights, because next time they might have to do the fighting themselves, which would not be the same thing at all. And there was a certain badger in the inn stables which had got to be released at once, and he'd come and see it done himself. Then he told them that the dragon had been thinking over things, and saw that there were two sides to every question, and he wasn't going to do it any more, and if they were good 'perhaps he'd stay and settle down there. So they must make friends, and not be prejudiced, and go about fancying they knew everything there was to be known, because they didn't, not by a long way. And he warned them against the sin of romancing, and making up stories and fancying other people would believe them just because they were plausible and highly-coloured. Then he sat down, amidst much repentant cheering, and the dragon nudged the Boy in the ribs and whispered that he couldn't have done it better himself. Then every one went off to get ready for the banquet.

Banquets are always pleasant things, consisting mostly, as they do, of eating and drinking;

but the specially nice thing about a banquet is, that it comes when something 's over, and there 's nothing more to worry about, and to-morrow seems a long way off. St. George was happy because there had been a fight and he had n't had to kill anybody; for he did n't really like killing, though he generally had to do it. The dragon was happy because there had been a fight, and so far from being hurt in it he had won popularity and a sure footing in society. The Boy was happy because there had been a fight, and in spite of it all his two friends were on the best of terms. And all the others were happy because there had been a fight, and — well, they did n't require any other reasons for their happiness. The dragon exerted himself to say the right thing to everybody, and proved the life and soul of the evening; while the Saint and the Boy, as they looked on, felt that they were only assisting at a feast of which the honour and the glory were entirely the dragon's. But they did n't mind that, being good fellows, and the dragon was not in the least proud or forgetful. On the contrary, every ten minutes or so he leant over towards the Boy and said impressively: "Look here! you *will* see me home afterwards, won't you?" And the Boy always nodded, though he had promised his mother not to be out late.

At last the banquet was over, the guests had dropped away with many good-nights and congratulations and invitations, and the dragon, who had seen the last of them off the premises, emerged into the street followed by the Boy, wiped his brow, sighed, sat down in the road and gazed at the stars. "Jolly night it's been!" he murmured. "Jolly stars! Jolly little place this! Think I shall just stop here. Don't feel like climbing up any beastly hill. Boy's promised to see me home. Boy had better do it then! No responsibility on my part. Responsibility all Boy's!" And his chin sank on his broad chest and he slumbered peacefully.

"Oh, *get* up, dragon," cried the Boy, piteously. "You *know* my mother's sitting up, and I'm so tired, and you made me promise to see you home, and I never knew what it meant or I would n't have done it!" And the Boy sat down in the road by the side of the sleeping dragon, and cried.

The door behind them opened, a stream of light illumined the road, and St. George, who had come out for a stroll in the cool night-air, caught sight of the two figures sitting there — the great motionless dragon and the tearful little Boy.

"What's the matter, Boy?" he inquired kindly, stepping to his side.

"Oh, it's this great lumbering *pig* of a dragon!" sobbed the Boy. "First he makes me promise to see him home, and then he says I'd better do it, and goes to sleep! Might as well try to see a *haystack* home! And I'm so tired, and mother's—" here he broke down again.

"Now don't take on," said St. George. "I'll stand by you, and we'll *both* see him home. Wake up, dragon!" he said sharply, shaking the beast by the elbow.

The dragon looked up sleepily. "What a night, George!" he murmured; "what a—"

"Now look here, dragon," said the Saint,

firmly. "Here's this little fellow waiting to
see you home, and you *know* he ought to have
been in bed these two hours, and what his
mother'll say *I* don't know, and anybody but
a selfish pig would have *made* him go to bed
long ago —"

"And he *shall* go to bed!" cried the dragon,
starting up. "Poor little chap, only fancy his
being up at this hour! It's a shame, that's
what it is, and I don't think, St. George, you've
been very considerate — but come along at once,
and don't let us have any more arguing or shilly-
shallying. You give me hold of your hand, Boy
— thank you, George, an arm up the hill is just
what I wanted!"

So they set off up the hill arm-in-arm, the
Saint, the Dragon, and the Boy. The lights
in the little village began to go out; but there
were stars, and a late moon, as they climbed to
the Downs together. And, as they turned the
last corner and disappeared from view, snatches
of an old song were borne back on the night-
breeze. I can't be certain which of them was
singing, but I *think* it was the Dragon!

" Here we are at your gate," said the man, abruptly, laying his hand on it. " Good-night. Cut along in sharp, or you 'll catch it ! "

Could it really be our own gate? Yes, there it was, sure enough, with the familiar marks on its bottom bar made by our feet when we swung on it.

" Oh, but wait a minute ! " cried Charlotte. " I want to know a heap of things. Did the dragon really settle down? And did — "

" There is n't any more of that story," said the man, kindly but firmly. " At least, not to-night. Now be off! Good-bye ! "

" Wonder if it 's all true? " said Charlotte, as we hurried up the path. " Sounded dread-fully like nonsense, in parts ! "

" P'raps it 's true for all that," I replied encouragingly.

Charlotte bolted in like a rabbit, out of the cold and the dark ; but I lingered a moment in the still, frosty air, for a backward glance at the silent white world without, ere I changed it for the land of firelight and cushions and laughter. It was the day for choir-practice, and caroltime

THE RELUCTANT DRAGON

was at hand, and a belated member was passing
homewards down the road, singing as he went: —

> " Then St. George : ee made rev'rence : in the stable so dim,
>   Oo vanquished the dragon : so fearful and grim.
>   So-o grim : and so-o fierce : that now may we say
>   All peaceful is our wakin' : on Chri-istmas Day ! "

The singer receded, the carol died away.   But
I wondered, with my hand on the door-latch,
whether that was the song, or something like it,
that the dragon sang as he toddled contentedly
up the hill.

A DEPARTURE

"As we turned to go, the man in the moon, tangled in elm
boughs, caught my eye for a moment."

A DEPARTURE

IT is a very fine thing to be a real Prince. There are points about a Pirate Chief, and to succeed to the Captaincy of a Robber Band is a truly magnificent thing. But to be an Heir has also about it something extremely captivating. Not only a long-lost heir — an heir of the melodrama, strutting into your hitherto unsuspected kingdom at just the right moment, loaded up with the consciousness of unguessed merit and of rights so long feloniously withheld — but even to be a common humdrum domestic heir is a profession to which few would refuse to be apprenticed. To step from leading-strings and restrictions and one glass of port after dinner, into property and liberty and due appreciation, saved up, polished and varnished, dusted and laid in lavender, all expressly for you — why, even the Princedom and the Robber Captaincy, when their anxieties and responsibilities are considered, have hardly more to offer. And so it will continue to be a problem, to the youth in whom ambition struggles with a certain sensuous appreciation of life's side-dishes, whether the career he is called upon to select out of the glittering knick-knacks that strew the counter had better be that of an heir or an engine-driver.

In the case of eldest sons, this problem has a way of solving itself. In childhood, however, the actual heirship is apt to work on the principle of the "Borough-English" of our happier ancestors, and in most cases of inheritance it is the youngest that succeeds. Where the "res" is "angusta," and the weekly books are simply a series of stiff hurdles at each of which in succession the paternal legs falter with growing suspicion of their powers to clear the flight, it is in the affair of *clothes* that the right of succession tells, and "the hard heir strides about the land" in trousers long ago framed for fraternal limbs—*frondes novas et non sua poma.* A bitter thing indeed! Of those pretty silken threads that knit humanity together, high and low, past and present, none is tougher, more pervading, or more iridescent, than the honest, simple pleasure of new clothes. It tugs at the man as it tugs at the woman ; the smirk of the well-fitted prince is no different from the smirk of the Sunday-clad peasant ; and the veins of the elders tingle with the same thrill that sets their fresh-frocked grandchildren skipping. Never trust people who pretend that they have no joy in their new clothes.

Let not our souls be wrung, however, at contemplation of the luckless urchin cut off by parental penury from the rapture of new clothes. Just as the heroes of his dreams are his immediate seniors, so his heroes' clothes share the glamour, and the reversion of them carries a high privilege — a special thing not sold by Swears and Wells. The sword of Galahad — and of many another hero — arrived on the scene already hoary with history, and the boy rather prefers his trousers to be legendary, famous, haloed by his hero's renown — even though the nap may have altogether vanished in the process.

But, putting clothes aside, there are other

matters in which this reversed heirship comes into play. Take the case of Toys. It is hardly right or fitting — and in this the child quite acquiesces — that as he approaches the reverend period of nine or say ten years, he should still be the unabashed and proclaimed possessor of a hoop and a Noah's Ark. The child will quite see the reasonableness of this, and, the goal of his ambition being now a catapult, a pistol, or even a sword-stick, will be satisfied that the titular ownership should lapse to his juniors, so far below him in their kilted or petticoated incompetence. After all, the things are still there, and if relapses of spirit occur, on wet afternoons, one can still (nominally) borrow them and be happy on the floor as of old, without the reproach of being a habitual baby toy-caresser. Also one can pretend it's being done to amuse the younger ones.

None of us, therefore, grumbled when in the natural course of things the nominal ownership of the toys slipped down to Harold, and from him in turn devolved upon Charlotte. The toys were still there; they always had been there and always would be there, and when the nursery door was fast shut there were no Kings or Queens or First Estates in that small Republic on the floor. Charlotte, to be sure, chin-tilted, at last an owner of real estate, might patronise a little at times; but it was tacitly understood that her "title" was only a drawing-room one.

Why does a coming bereavement project no thin faint voice, no shadow of its woe, to warn its happy, heedless victims? Why cannot Olympians ever think it worth while to give some hint of the thunderbolts they are silently forging? And why, oh, why did it never enter any of our thick heads that the day would come when even Charlotte would be considered too matronly for toys? One's so-called education is hammered into one with rulers and with canes. Each fresh grammar or musical instrument, each new historical period or quaint arithmetical rule, is impressed on one by some painful physical prelude. Why does Time, the biggest Schoolmaster, alone neglect premonitory raps, at each stage of his curriculum, on our knuckles or our heads?

Uncle Thomas was at the bottom of it. This

was not the first mine he had exploded under our bows. In his favourite pursuit of fads he had passed in turn from Psychical Research to the White Rose and thence to a Children's Hospital, and we were being daily inundated with leaflets headed by a woodcut depicting Little Annie (of Poplar) sitting up in her little white cot, surrounded by the toys of the nice, kind, rich children. The idea caught on with the Olympians, always open to sentiment of a treacly, woodcut order; and accordingly Charlotte, on entering one day dishevelled and panting, having been pursued by yelling Redskins up to the very threshold of our peaceful home, was curtly informed that her French lessons would begin on Monday, that she was henceforth to cease all pretence of being a trapper or a Redskin on utterly inadequate grounds, and moreover that the whole of her toys were at that moment being finally packed up in a box, for despatch to London, to gladden the lives and bring light into the eyes of London waifs and Poplar Annies.

Naturally enough, perhaps, we others received

no official intimation of this grave cession of territory. We were not supposed to be interested. Harold had long ago been promoted to a knife — a recognised, birthday knife. As for me, it was known that I was already given over, heart and soul, to lawless abandoned catapults — catapults which were confiscated weekly for reasons of international complications, but with which Edward kept me steadily supplied, his school having a fine old tradition for excellence in their manufacture. Therefore no one was supposed to be really affected but Charlotte, and even she had already reached Miss Yonge, and should therefore have been more interested in prolific curates and harrowing deathbeds.

Notwithstanding, we all felt indignant, betrayed, and sullen to the verge of mutiny. Though for long we had affected to despise them, these toys, yet they had grown up with us, shared our joys and our sorrows, seen us at our worst, and become part of the accepted scheme of existence. As we gazed at untenanted shelves and empty, hatefully tidy corners, perhaps for the first time for long we began to do them a tardy justice.

There was old Leotard, for instance. Somehow he had come to be sadly neglected of late years — and yet how exactly he always responded to certain moods! He was an acrobat, this Leotard, who lived in a glass-fronted box. His loose-jointed limbs were cardboard, cardboard his slender trunk; and his hands eternally grasped the bar of a trapeze. You turned the box round swiftly five or six times; the wonderful unsolved machinery worked, and Leotard swung and leapt, backwards, forwards, now astride the bar, now flying free; iron-jointed, supple-sinewed, unceasingly novel in his invention of new, unguessable attitudes; while above, below, and around him, a richly-dressed audience, painted in skilful perspective of stalls, boxes, dress-circle, and gallery, watched the thrilling performance with a stolidity which seemed to mark them out as made in Germany. Hardly versatile enough, perhaps, this Leotard; unsympathetic, not a companion for all hours; nor would you have chosen him to take to bed with you. And yet, within his own limits, how fresh, how engrossing, how resourceful and inventive! Well, he was

gone, it seemed — merely gone. Never specially
cherished while he tarried with us, he had yet
contrived to build himself a particular niche of
his own. Sunrise and sunset, and the dinner-bell,
and the sudden rainbow, and lessons, and Leotard,
and the moon through the nursery windows — they
were all part of the great order of things, and
the displacement of any one item seemed to dis-
organise the whole machinery. The immediate
point was, not that the world would continue to
go round as of old, but that Leotard would n't.

Yonder corner, now swept and garnished, had
been the stall wherein the spotty horse, at the
close of each laborious day, was accustomed to
doze peacefully the long night through. In
days of old each of us in turn had been jerked
thrillingly round the room on his precarious
back, had dug our heels into his unyielding
sides, and had scratched our hands on the tin
tacks that secured his mane to his stiffly-curving
neck. Later, with increasing stature, we came
to overlook his merits as a beast of burden ; but
how frankly, how good-naturedly, he had recognised the new conditions, and adapted himself

to them without a murmur! When the military spirit was abroad, who so ready to be a squadron of cavalry, a horde of Cossacks, or artillery pounding into position? He had even served with honour as a gun-boat, during a period when naval strategy was the only theme; and no false equine pride ever hindered him from taking the part of a roaring locomotive, earth-shaking, clangorous, annihilating time and space. Really it was no longer clear how life, with its manifold emergencies, was to be carried on at all without a fellow like the spotty horse, ready to step in at critical moments and take up just the part required of him.

In moments of mental depression, nothing is quite so consoling as the honest smell of a painted animal; and mechanically I turned towards the shelf that had been so long the Ararat of our weather-beaten Ark. The shelf was empty, the Ark had cast off moorings and sailed away to Poplar, and had taken with it its haunting smell, as well as that pleasant sense of disorder that the best conducted Ark is always able to impart. The sliding roof had rarely been known to close entirely. There was always a pair of giraffe-legs sticking out, or an elephant-trunk, taking from the stiffness of its outline, and reminding us that our motley crowd of friends inside were uncomfortably cramped for room and only too ready to leap in a cascade on the floor and browse and gallop, flutter and bellow and neigh, and be their natural selves again. I think that none of us ever really thought very much of Ham and Shem and Japhet. They were only there because they were in the story, but nobody really wanted them. The Ark was built for the animals, of course — animals with tails, and trunks, and horns, and at least three legs apiece, though some unfortunates had been unable to retain even that number. And in the animals were of course included the birds — the dove, for instance, grey with black wings, and the red-crested woodpecker — or was it a hoopoe? — and the insects, for there was a dear beetle, about the same size as the dove, that held its own with any of the mammalia.

Of the doll-department Charlotte had naturally been sole chief for a long time; if the staff were

not in their places to-day, it was not I who had
any official right to take notice. And yet one
may have been member of a Club for many a
year without ever exactly understanding the use
and object of the other members, until one enters,
some Christmas day or other holiday, and, survey-
ing the deserted armchairs, the untenanted sofas,
the barren hat-pegs, realises, with depression, that
those other fellows had their allotted functions,
after all. Where was old Jerry? Where were
Eugenie, Rosa, Sophy, Esmeralda? We had
long drifted apart, it was true, we spoke but
rarely; perhaps, absorbed in new ambitions,
new achievements, I had even come to look
down on these conservative, unprogressive members who were so clearly content to remain simply
what they were. And now that their corners
were unfilled, their chairs unoccupied — well,
my eyes were opened and I wanted 'em back!

However it was no business of mine. If
grievances were the question, I had n't a leg to
stand upon. Though my catapults were officially confiscated, I knew the drawer in which
they were incarcerated, and where the key of it

was hidden, and I could make life a burden, if I chose, to every living thing within a square-mile radius, so long as the catapult was restored to its drawer in due and decent time. But I wondered how the others were taking it. The edict hit them more severely. They should have my moral countenance at any rate, if not more, in any protest or countermine they might be planning. And, indeed, something seemed possible, from the dogged, sullen air with which the two of them had trotted off in the direction of the raspberry-canes. Certain spots always had their insensible attraction for certain moods. In love, one sought the orchard. Weary of discipline, sick of convention, impassioned for the road, the mining-camp, the land across the border, one made for the big meadow. Mutinous, sulky, charged with plots and conspiracies, one always got behind the shelter of the raspberry-canes.

.   .   .   .

" You can come too if you like," said Harold, in a subdued sort of way, as soon as he was aware that I was sitting up in bed watching him.

" We did n't think you 'd care, 'cos you 've got to catapults. But we 're goin' to do what we 've settled to do, so it 's no good sayin' we had n't ought and that sort of thing, 'cos we 're goin' to ! "

The day had passed in an ominous peacefulness. Charlotte and Harold had kept out of my way, as well as out of everybody else's, in a purposeful manner that ought to have bred suspicion. In the evening we had read books, or fitfully drawn ships and battles on fly-leaves, apart, in separate corners, void of conversation or criticism, oppressed by the lowering tidiness of the universe, till bedtime came, and disrobement, and prayers even more mechanical than usual, and lastly bed itself without so much as a giraffe under the pillow. Harold had grunted himself between the sheets with an ostentatious pretence of overpowering fatigue ; but I noticed that he pulled his pillow forward and propped his head against the brass bars of his crib, and, as I was acquainted with most of his tricks and subterfuges, it was easy for me to gather that a painful wakefulness was his aim that night.

A DEPARTURE

I had dozed off, however, and Harold was out and on his feet, poking under the bed for his shoes, when I sat up and grimly regarded him. Just as he said I could come if I liked, Charlotte slipped in, her face rigid and set. And then it was borne in upon me that I was not on in this scene. These youngsters had planned it all out, the piece was their own, and the mounting, and the cast. My sceptre had fallen, my rule had ceased. In this magic hour of the summer night laws went for nothing, codes were cancelled, and those who were most in touch with the moonlight and the warm June spirit and the topsy-turvydom that reigns when the clock strikes ten, were the true lords and lawmakers.

Humbly, almost timidly, I followed without a protest in the wake of these two remorseless, purposeful young persons, who were marching straight for the schoolroom. Here in the moonlight the grim big box stood visible — the box in which so large a portion of our past and our personality lay entombed, cold, swathed in paper, awaiting the carrier of the morning who should speed them forth to the strange, cold, distant Children's Hospital, where their little failings would all be misunderstood and no one would make allowances. A dreamy spectator, I stood idly by while Harold propped up the lid and the two plunged in their arms and probed and felt and grappled.

"Here's Rosa," said Harold, suddenly. "I know the feel of her hair. Will you have Rosa out?"

"Oh, give me Rosa!" cried Charlotte, with a sort of gasp. And when Rosa had been dragged forth, quite unmoved apparently, placid as ever in her moonfaced contemplation of this comedy-world with its ups and downs, Charlotte retired with her to the window-seat, and there in the moonlight the two exchanged their private confidences, leaving Harold to his exploration alone.

"Here's something with sharp corners," said Harold, presently. "Must be Leotard, I think. Better let *him* go."

"Oh, yes, we can't save Leotard," assented Charlotte, limply.

Poor old Leotard ! I said nothing, of course ;
I was not on in this piece. But, surely, had
Leotard heard and rightly understood all that
was going on above him, he must have sent up
one feeble, strangled cry, one faint appeal to be
rescued from unfamiliar little Annies and retained
for an audience certain to appreciate and never
unduly critical.

"Now I've got to the Noah's Ark," panted
Harold, still groping blindly.

"Try and shove the lid back a bit," said
Charlotte, "and pull out a dove or a zebra or
a giraffe if there's one handy."

Harold toiled on with grunts and contortions,
and presently produced in triumph a small grey
elephant and a large beetle with a red stomach.

"They're jammed in too tight," he com-
plained. "Can't get any more out. But as I
came up I'm sure I felt Potiphar!" And down
he dived again.

Potiphar was a finely modelled bull with a
suède skin, rough and comfortable and warm in
bed. He was my own special joy and pride,
and I thrilled with honest emotion when Poti-

phar emerged to light once more, stout-necked
and stalwart as ever.

"That'll have to do," said Charlotte, getting
up. "We durs n't take any more, 'cos we'll be
found out if we do. Make the box all right,
and bring 'em along."

Harold rammed down the wads of paper and
twists of straw he had disturbed, replaced the
lid squarely and innocently, and picked up his
small salvage; and we sneaked off for the window most generally in use for prison-breakings
and nocturnal escapades. A few seconds later
and we were hurrying silently in single file along
the dark edge of the lawn.

Oh, the riot, the clamour, the crowding chorus,
of all silent things that spoke by scent and colour
and budding thrust and foison, that moonlit night
of June! Under the laurel-shade all was still
ghostly enough, brigand-haunted, crackling,
whispering of night and all its possibilities of
terror. But the open garden, when once we
were in it — how it turned a glad new face to
welcome us, glad as of old when the sunlight
raked and searched it, new with the unfamiliar

night-aspect that yet welcomed us as guests to a hall where the horns blew up to a new, strange banquet! Was this the same grass, could these be the same familiar flower-beds, alleys, clumps of verdure, patches of sward? At least this full white light that was flooding them was new, and accounted for all. It was Moonlight Land, and Past-Ten-o'clock Land, and we were in it and of it, and all its other denizens fully understood, and, tongue-free and awakened at last, responded and comprehended and knew. The other two, doubtless, hurrying forward full of their mission, noted little of all this. I, who was only a super, had leisure to take it all in, and, though the language and the message of the land were not all clear to me then, long afterwards I remembered and understood.

Under the farthest hedge, at the loose end of things, where the outer world began with the paddock, there was darkness once again — not the blackness that crouched so solidly under the crowding laurels, but a duskiness hung from far-spread arms of high-standing elms. There, where the small grave made a darker spot on

the grey, I overtook them, only just in time to
see Rosa laid stiffly out, her cherry cheeks pale
in the moonlight, but her brave smile triumphant
and undaunted as ever. It was a tiny grave
and a shallow one, to hold so very much. Rosa
once in, Potiphar, who had hitherto stood erect,
stout-necked, through so many days and such
various weather, must needs bow his head and
lie down meekly on his side. The elephant and
the beetle, equal now in a silent land where a
vertebra and a red circulation counted for nothing, had to snuggle down where best they might,
only a little less crowded than in their native
Ark.

The earth was shovelled in and stamped down,
and I was glad that no orisons were said and no
speechifying took place. The whole thing was
natural and right and self explanatory, and needed
no justifying or interpreting to our audience of
stars and flowers. The connexion was not entirely broken now — one link remained between
us and them. The Noah's Ark, with its cargo
of sad-faced emigrants, might be hull down on
the horizon, but two of its passengers had missed

the boat and would henceforth be always near us ; and, as we played above them, an elephant would understand, and a beetle would hear, and crawl again in spirit along a familiar floor. Henceforth the spotty horse would scour along far-distant plains and know the homesickness of alien stables ; but Potiphar, though never again would he paw the arena when bull-fights were on the bill, was spared maltreatment by town-bred strangers, quite capable of mistaking him for a cow. Jerry and Esmeralda might shed their limbs and their stuffing, by slow or swift degrees, in uttermost parts and unguessed corners of the globe ; but Rosa's book was finally closed, and no worse fate awaited her than natural dissolution almost within touch and hail of familiar faces and objects that had been friendly to her since first she opened her eyes on a world where she had never been treated as a stranger.

As we turned to go, the man in the moon, tangled in elm-boughs, caught my eye for a moment, and I thought that never had he looked so friendly. He was going to see after them, it was evident ; for he was always there, more or less, and it was no trouble to him at all, and he would tell them how things were still going, up here, and throw in a story or two of his own whenever they seemed a trifle dull. It made the going away rather easier, to know one had left somebody behind on the spot ; a good fellow, too, cheery, comforting, with a fund of anecdote ; a man in whom one had every confidence.

BOOKS BY KENNETH GRAHAME

D R E A M   D A Y S

THE OUTLOOK. — 'Nobody with a sense of what is rare and humorous and true can afford to miss this volume.'

LITERATURE. — 'In "Dream Days" we are conscious of the same magic touch which charmed us in "The Golden Age." There is magic in all the sketches, but it is perhaps in "Its Walls were as of Jasper" — the beautiful title of a beautiful story — that Mr. Grahame stands confessed as a veritable wizard.'

THE DAILY TELEGRAPH. — 'Happy Mr. Grahame, who can weave romances so well.'

THE WORLD. — 'Could only have been written by a poet full of happy imaginings, quaint conceits, and a certain winsome waywardness which has a charm of its own. . . . The closing chapter is full of a tenderness and reticent pathos far above anything the author has yet achieved. It is certainly a book to be read, for it would be a pity to miss the many exquisite passages it contains.'

THE DAILY MAIL. — 'Mr. Grahame's book will bring youth and joy into many a jaded heart.'

T H E   H E A D S W O M A N

THE BOOKMAN. — 'Mr. Grahame's cleverness does not forsake him when he attempts satire. "The Headswoman" is a pretty bit of foolery.'

THE LITERARY WORLD. — 'A delightful little tale with a tinge of satire in it. For gracefulness of style and charm in the telling of a story it is in the front rank, and that is saying a great deal.'

MR. W. L. COURTNEY IN DAILY TELEGRAPH. — 'Well, we are more than a trifle dull, *nous autres ;* and we should be grateful to Mr. Kenneth Grahame for throwing in a story or two of his own as often as he can. Happy Mr. Grahame, who can weave romances so well.'

THE DUNDEE ADVERTISER. — 'Humour is not dead amongst us, for Kenneth Grahame's witty little romance of "The Headswoman" brims over with it.'

THE SCOTSMAN. — 'Mr. Grahame has written a most charming book, which cannot fail to delight all who were once children.'

JOHN LANE · THE BODLEY HEAD
LONDON AND NEW YORK

EVELYN SHARP'S FAIRY-BOOKS

ROUND THE WORLD TO WYMPLAND
ILLUSTRATED BY ALICE B. WOODWARD

THE OTHER SIDE OF THE SUN
ILLUSTRATED BY NELLIE SYRETT

ALL THE WAY TO FAIRYLAND
ILLUSTRATED BY MRS. PERCY DEARMER

WYMPS
ILLUSTRATED BY MRS. PERCY DEARMER

THE ST. JAMES'S GAZETTE. — 'To be able to write a good fairy tale is given to few, though alas! a good many incompetent people imagine they are able to do so. Far and away the best fairy tales are the old traditional stories of Cinderella, Jack and the Beanstalk, and others. To these we add the stories of Hans Andersen and Grimm; and now room must be made in that select company for the tales of Evelyn Sharp. In her books children will find unmixed delight. The tales are genuine fairy tales; they abound in quaint conceits, happy devices, fun, wit, and real wisdom, and every one of the tales is in such simple language that a child of eight (as we have proved) can understand and enjoy them.'

P. J. BILLINGHURST'S FABLE-BOOKS

A HUNDRED FABLES OF ÆSOP

With 101 full-page illustrations by PERCY J. BILLING-HURST, and a fifteen-page introduction including two new and original fables by KENNETH GRAHAME.

A HUNDRED FABLES OF LA FONTAINE

With 101 full-page illustrations by PERCY J. BILLING-HURST.

In *La Fontaine's Fables,* Mr. Billinghurst's delightful animals pose and strut and swagger in the same powerful and moral-mending manner that they did in his Æsop. — KENNETH GRAHAME in *Daily Mail.*

A HUNDRED ANECDOTES OF ANIMALS

With 102 full-page illustrations by PERCY J. BILLING-HURST.

It is a treasure-house of natural history anecdotes, sumptuously illustrated in black and white, and serves both to arouse and stimulate interest in the subject in children of a knowledgeable age.